The Womb
Rebellion

To Maguire,
Discover the "Ruby" with in you!!!

p.w. long

biredagrp5 @ yahoo. com

blue ocean press

tokyo – florida

Published by:
blue ocean press, an imprint of Aoishima Research Institute

U.S. (Main) Office
P.O. Box 510818
Punta Gorda, Florida 33951

807-36 Lions Plaza Ebisu
3-25-3 Higashi, Shibuya-ku, Tokyo, Japan 150

Email: contact@blueoceanpublications.com
URL: http://www.blueoceanpublications.com

ISBN: 978-4-902837-90-2

Cover Art by MaryRose Arciero

Table of Contents

Dedicated To:

Great-great grandmother, Martha Baker,

Great-great grandmother, Martha Williams

Great-grand mother, Priscilla Long, midwife.

Acknowledgements

While writing a book is a solitary task, it is never done without the voices, muses, inspiration, and encouragement of ancestors, family, and very special friends. I wish to thank my daughter Saba, and son-in-law Emanuel for their love and encouragement in all of my endeavors. A special thank-you to my grandson, Nahom for his inspiration by simply being in my life.

Thank you to my dear friend and writing muse, Myrna Charry for her constant support of my writing. Thank you to my special friend and the best editor I could ever have, Colleen O'Brien, my "Sista Col".

And, a very heartfelt thank you to the person whose persistent inspiration, guidance, and work on my behalf brought this book into fruition, my son. Jaha Cummings. Jaha, thank you for your love, support, and belief in me and in the voices of the women whose story is told in this book.

Finally, a thank-you to Delores Newton for permission to use portions of the poem written by her mother Jane Newton in this book. The poem eloquently in a few verses goes to the heart of this work.

Prologue – 1913

My people believe that death comes in threes, but this was the strangest coincidence I have seen. I went home for the funeral of my aunt Ruby Pearl Clark. That very same weekend Ruby Grace Jones died, and only two weeks before, Ruby Ann Taylor had passed away. As my mother talked to me about them all dying, I inquired of my mother how these three women all the same age came to be named Ruby.

She let out a guffaw and told me to have a seat. "What your grandma told me was that after the War, they all named their first baby girl in honor of a rebellious young slave named Ruby. But your aunt bore the name of both Ruby and Pearl -- the midwife who grandma said led some kind of revolt -- the women refused to have babies."

"Mama, this is the most exciting thing I've ever heard. You mean a slave owner couldn't make his slave women have children? And some midwife led them?"

"That's the story your grandma and the women in Bellamy Place tell."

"Is the midwife still alive? Does she live right here in Bellamy Place?"

"As far as I know she is still living. But Grandma said she moved to Florida with her husband after the War."

"Where in Florida? How can I find her? I want to know more."

I asked everyone who lived on Bellamy Place what they knew about Pearl the midwife and the young Ruby. Two months later, I received a letter about a Mrs. Pearl Lancaster. I wrote to her that my aunt Ruby Pearl, whom she might have helped bring into this life, had recently died, and I was curious to know if it was true that the enslaved women on Bellamy Plantation refused to have children. She replied that, yes, despite lashings and the threat of being sold South, the women bravely and stubbornly endured. In my next letter, I asked permission to interview her about the events that took place on Bellamy Plantation in the 1850s and '60s. She agreed, and I was soon on my way to Greenwood, Florida, to visit the now-100-year-old Pearl Lancaster, midwife of Bellamy.

A grass- and dirt-covered path lined with sea shells and a parade of red, yellow and purple flowers led up to Mrs. Lancaster's home, one of a half-dozen neat cottages set back from the road. A small tree hung with blue bottles stood prominently in the front yard of the small white house with the blue shutters. On the front porch sat two pine rocking chairs.

As I approached the door, it opened and I was met with a warm hello by a young woman who introduced herself as Liza. She invited me into the small living room where the smell of lavender filled my nostrils. The room was classily appointed -- lace curtains at the three windows, a wine-colored sofa with white crocheted coverlets on the back and arms, two straight-backed chairs, a small serving table. In front of a brick fireplace sat two rocking chairs draped with many-colored crocheted throws, oil lamps sat on either end of the mantle where a vase filled with sunflowers stood next to a bouquet of dried lavender tied with a red ribbon.

Appearing from a room to the right came an older woman, beautiful and looking at least 20 years younger than her age, which I knew to be a hundred. She was elegant in a high-necked blue dress with lace collar and a string of pearls, her gray hair pulled into a bun.

"You must be Carrie Telfair," she said to me. "I am Pearl Lancaster."

"Yes, ma'am, so pleased to meet you," I said, standing and extending my hand.

"I am saddened by the death of your aunt Ruby Pearl. She was the prettiest baby born that year after the war, such a fine time that was. I saw her grow up, you know, a smart and determined young woman."

She looked me in the eye and said, "So you have heard of the story of the women on Bellamy Plantati." She had a wry smile.

"Yes, ma'am. I am excited to hear more."

"Please have a seat, Miss Telfair." Mrs. Lancaster sat on the divan, crossing her legs at the ankle, hands folded gracefully in her lap. I found myself copying her pose. "The women slaves stood on the principle that no human being should own another person and that no child should be born into slavery," she said calmly. "They had a saying: 'Massa may own me and my labor, but he doesn't own this. All that I own is this here." She held her long-fingered hands across her belly.

Everything about Mrs. Lancaster surprised me, from her house to herself. Her voice was soft, with quiet determination. Her light complexion and green eyes were not the image I'd held in my mind of a slave midwife; I thought I would be meeting a dark-brown-skinned plump woman wearing a scarf wrapped around her head like a turban.

As if reading my thoughts, she said, "Not quite who you expected?" She smiled at me and said to her companion, "Liza, please bring our guest lemonade and tea cakes.

"Wouldn't any of this ever come to be without my dear sweet Ruby," she said, starting off abruptly again with her story. "She was like a daughter to me. What a rebellious child, never meant to be a slave." She interrupted herself to summon Liza again. "Get my wrap, please, honey." My gaze followed Liza into the bedroom. "You can go in, see the old woman's room, I don't mind," Mrs. Lancaster said. "That was my and Joseph's room before he died. Liza has her own room."

I followed Liza into the small bedroom with the white metal bed, crocheted white bedspread and all-white crazy quilt on top. A small dresser sat in the corner; there was a nightstand with an oil lamp and a white and pink porcelain basin, beside it a white chamber pot. The smell of lavender filled this room also. On top of the dresser was a photo of a Union soldier.

"Handsome, isn't he?" Mrs. Lancaster said from the front room. "He was free, joined the

Union Army in Philadelphia. I met him in 1865 when the War was over. There were colored troops everywhere on the islands. All the whites had gone. Mr. Bellamy and the overseer went to war and Miss Bellamy left for somewhere. The whole quarters moved into the Big House, had us a ball. The cook still prepared meals, but this time it was the slaves who were eating ham and biscuits. I still have china and silver the women brought to me, thanking me for being the midwife."

A look of pride washed over her gentle face. "You know, a midwife had a special place in the quarters. Being a midwife is a gift from God. I brought more babies into this world...." She laughed. "Especially after the War. Seemed like every colored woman I knew was pregnant. Those were the best times for me, bringing free children into the world.

"There were always more women than men on Bellamy Plantation," Mrs. Lancaster continued. "After they made it illegal to import slaves from Africa, 1807 or 1808, sometime in there, the planters started breeding slaves just like you do cattle. It was terrible, and I was caught up in the middle of it. Put women with just any man they felt could produce strong, healthy children. The female babies with

12

white blood were especially valuable for places like New Orleans, so the Master made the women mate with white men he would invite to dinner parties.

"One thing I can say about Bellamy, though, he wouldn't sell any slave with Bellamy blood. Gave them the best jobs on the plantation -- made them driver, put them in the Big House, even taught them to read and write, though it was against the law. Yes, I've got Bellamy blood in me.

"Ben, the Master, or Massa, as we slaves pronounced it, was my brother." She stopped and coughed slightly. "I'm glad a colored girl is interested in my story. Our young people need to know that we women protested slavery in our own special way.

"I know you're here to interview me, but this is Ruby's story, that of my adopted daughter, who refused to accept slavery as her identity or her destiny. And it is also the story of the women on Bellamy Plantation who were empowered by Ruby's courageous action."

Carrie Telfair, September 1913

Book I
1843–1859

"If you would wear a red gown,
Waste no time being old;
Black is for the wise ones,
Crimson for the bold."

Jane Newton

Ruby's Birth

The room is dark except for the dying embers in the fireplace. 1 wonder if I should throw another log or two on to keep the cabin warm through the night. But I am snug and do not want to get up, so I decide that the place is warm enough and I bury my head beneath the quilts. "Too tired to do anything more this day," I say to myself and drift off into a deep sleep. It seems as though I have just gone under when I am awakened by frantic banging on my cabin door.

"Pearl, git up quick. Mintaa 'bout to have dis baby." It is Buck, Mintaa's brother, desperate like most men when it comes to new babies.

I place my feet on the cold floor and stand up in the now freezing room and stumble over to let him in. "Ouch! It's cold in here! I'm coming!"

"She havin' a hard time, Sistah Pearl. Say dis baby sumtin' else. Please, come quick!"

"I'm coming now, just let me get my things." I shoo him out and turn to get dressed. "Heat some water right away," I yell at him. "Make the birth fire and then gather the women."

Shivering from the cold I pull on my gray birthing smock and grab my fresh white apron. With my bag used for deliveries, I head out the door. The night air is frigid and frost has settled on the ground. Shrinking into the quilt around my shoulders I scurry down the street to Mintaa's. Warm air greets me in the over-heated cabin. In the corner sits the ancient blind slave Mina, whose lips move in one of her strange chants. The fireplace is aglow and women busy themselves -- Bina making tea, Hannah laying out the birthing pallet, Sally preparing a bath for the baby. Birthing babies in the quarters is women's work, and all of the women gather to assist. Each takes a task and offers comfort to the mother during the labor. Afterward, they clean and grease the baby and take part in the ritual to bury the afterbirth. I smile and say to myself, "I love birthin' time."

"Sista Pearl, dis baby, she different," whispers an exhausted Mintaa.

"How do you know it's a girl?"

"You know, too, look where I been carryin' her, way up high. A real strange feeling I hab. Seem like dis baby don't care 'bout being born. Bin sick de whole time. Tot I was gon lose her once. I think she wanna be wid Chike."

Chike, Mintaa's husband and the baby's father, died before knowing that his wife was carrying a child. He had been a slave who often refused to work. The last time, he was beaten almost to death by the overseer. Mintaa and her family tried to nurse him back to health, but according to Mintaa, "His spirit jus' choose to return home. Ya know he be Ibo, and dem Ibos don' do well wit bein' a slave."

It was at Ibo Landing in the early 1800s where a tribal group of enslaved Ibos committed mass suicide. Chained together they walked right into the river and drowned. Chike liked to talk about the bravery of those men and the unwillingness of Ibos to be bound.

"Ah, Mintaa, don't think about that. You will be fine. Let's get you up and walking so we can bring this along." I help Mintaa to rise from the chair, place an arm around her waist, my other hand on her belly and gently walk her back and forth in the small, now very crowded cabin. The women part as we move slowly. I massage Mintaa's shoulders and back and whisper encouraging words into her ear while even more women come in to help with the birth.

"Mintaa, you are just scared because it is your first time. When you do this again, it will be easier."

"Don't believe dat, always hard," teases Sally. "But you be alright. Can't make dem pains go away but we all here for you."

Mintaa smiles but immediately a pain hits her so hard it takes her breath away.

"Pearl, help me!" Mintaa doubles over. I get her to the pallet on the floor and gently help her to kneel and then to lie on her side. "Just rest here for a few minutes." I gently brush her hair from her forehead. l rub her abdomen with castor oil and lard and gently massage her to position the baby for birth." It's almost time."

After a few minutes, I tell her, "Let me help you to kneel up here now, pull your knees apart. Hold tight to the back of this chair and push when its time." I help her onto two cushions covered with mats made of medicinal herbs, and two of the women stand on either side of the chair to hold it steady. As Mintaa kneels, Bina sits behind her and holds her up by clasping her under her arms. Others kneel near the pallet, ready to do what I say. l stay beside her as Sally gently rubs her back and Hannah places hot cloths on her forehead.

"Ugh, oh my God!" screams Mintaa.

I place my ear on Mintaa's belly and gently feel for the position of the baby.

I see the women widen their eyes, and I realize I am incautious and have allowed my distress to cross my face. I take a deep breath.

"She hasn't turned yet. You might be right, Mintaa. This one is going to need some help."

Mintaa screams and struggles, I gently massage her belly and whisper to her, "Relax. Everything will be alright. She's coming."

"No, Pearl, I got a bad feelin', dis baby don' wants to be born," sighs Mintaa.

No matter how much I massage Mintaa's belly, the baby will not turn, but at long last starts to come out, backwards, feet first. I am churning inside and sweat pours down my face. Sally continually wipes my forehead. My mind races. *How can I get the shoulders out without damaging the mother or having the cord strangle the baby?*

I pray out loud, "Lord help me, please! Help me! Show me how to do this!"

The women all start to pray out loud as well. "Lord! Help Sista Pearl delibber dis baby. Thank you, Lord!" they shout. "Sista Pearl, God is wid you. Hab faith!"

They pray. The baby's legs are now visible. I take a deep breath and gently but forcefully place my hands within Mintaa's birth canal. I feel to find the shoulders and when I am sure that the cord is not around the baby's neck, I shout, "Now push, Mintaa, push!"

But as I tell Mintaa to push, I feel something I have never encountered. As I tug to help the baby emerge, the baby seems to physically resist my efforts.

I and the baby are engaged in a tug of war.

"Let go! Let go!" I yell. The struggling mother and wide-eyed women are confused by my screams. It seems the more I try, the more the child resists. Finally I scream at the top of my lungs to Mintaa "Push! Push! Push!"

Mintaa pushes and finally the shoulders, neck, and head of the baby emerge. Confused and weary, 1 collapse on the floor beside the pallet. Hannah takes the baby and begins to clean and oil her as Bina cuts the cord. The baby lets out a sound that neither I nor the women have ever heard before; a sad wail like a mourn of grief. This is not the usual boisterous announcement of a child just born.

I turn my attention back to Mintaa who is now bleeding heavily. I vigorously massage her belly so that the afterbirth will soon be born as well. "Get me clean rags quickly," I say. "And look in my bag, get the herbs in the little brown pouch, use them to make tea to give to Mintaa."

"Let me see my girl," Mintaa moans. Hannah gently lifts the oiled purple-reddish baby onto Mintaa's bosom. "Here she is. See, you dun do it. You got yorself a baby girl."

"Ah, she pretty, jus' like a jewel." Mintaa tries to place the newborn to her breast, but the baby turns her tiny head away. "I tol' you, Pearl, dis chile gon be trouble, she don wanna come here," Mintaa says with great sadness in her weak voice.

"Mintaa, give her time," I say. "Stroke her little cheek like this." I gently touch the baby's soft skin. "Now let us work on you, get you better." But even as I encourage Mintaa, the thoughts and feelings of the child struggling and resisting being born flood my mind.

I deliver the afterbirth, and Bina salts it. She and several women take it outside to bury it with ceremony near a tree in the icy backyard. Mintaa continues to bleed.

Despite giving the special tea, keeping the fire in the fireplace as hot as possible, and massaging her belly, her condition deteriorates. Mintaa grows weaker and weaker. She gestures for me to come closer.

"Look out for my baby. She special. She ain't like de rest a us. Name my li'l jewel Ruby when it time." With that, Mintaa breathes her last and dies.

~~~

The baby is now passed woman to woman; each holds her and whispers into her ear. The tiny naked thing is finally handed to the old blind woman, Mina, sitting in the corner. She takes the baby, holds her above her head, and mumbles words foreign to my ears. She holds the baby close to her bosom and chants to her.

I am so exhausted I can hardly stand, but my heart is pounding, and troubling thoughts about old Mina race through my mind. *Why does she have to be here? Why this birth? She seldom makes the effort. This is the most difficult birth that I have ever helped with: a child who fought being born and a mother who has just taken her last breath. I am embarrassed that the old women witnessed me.*

Tears stream down my face as I feel a pang of loss and helplessness I have never experienced before. The women gather round. Bina and Hannah put their arms around me and hold me close, murmuring in my ear. "Dis be God's will for Mintaa to go, she

gon to join Chike." "You save de baby." "God lookin'
over you and dat chile." "You go on home now,
Sista Pearl, we finish here."

Bina and Hannah gather my bag and place
my cloak around me. "Flora gon take dis baby and
try to feed her. You git some res'. Dis been a long
night."

I kiss each woman on the cheek and leave. As
I walk along the icy path, I am shivering, but it is not
from the cold. I sit up in my bed in my freezing
cabin, unable to sleep throughout the remaining
hours before sunrise. I am unnerved. Most troubling,
the mother has given me the overwhelming
responsibility to care for her child. The weight of this
request sits on my heart. *How does one protect an
enslaved child?* Mintaa's last plea turns me to anger.
*There are many women in the quarters who have
lost children and would take care of this one. Why
not them? Why me? I caught your child, placed her
on your breast, and tried to save your life.* "Why
have you cursed me with this task?" I say to my cabin
walls. W*early, I wonder, What does this all mean?*

Never before have I undergone something as
strange as a baby pulling back into the womb.

Nine Days

The squalor and the overbearing heat of Flora's cabin overwhelm me each time I visit. She sits topless, cloth covering her legs, a baby on each breast. Her own baby Sukie tugs vigorously while the other lies eyes wide, lips tightly pursed. This is the child who will be called Ruby if she survives the nine days the quarters believes is a message from the Creator that the child is meant to live,

"Sis Pearl, I afraid dis baby ain't gon make it. She don' want de breast. I tries and tries but she won' suck. I rubs her jaw gently, teases her lips, but nuthin' works. What I gon do?"

I reach down and kiss the forehead of the resistant baby. Her big brown eyes catch mine; puzzlement is the only emotion that they betray. A tinge of doubt shakes me. *Should I have tried so hard to save her? She does not seem to want to live.*

"Just keep trying, Flora. If she doesn't suck, she won't survive," I say dejectedly. This is the third day that I have received the same news. "I will be back after I check on the others." I rush out of the cabin.

Coming up the quarter's street is Miss Charlotte, mistress of the plantation, who likes to keep check on all of the new babies born in the quarters.

"How is our new one?" she asks cheerfully and hopefully.

"She is still not sucking. Flora is trying everything," I reply.

Miss Charlotte frowns. "Well, we will just have to find a way to force some nourishment into that little stubborn mouth of hers. Can't have her starving herself, can we?"

"No, Miss Charlotte, we won't let her starve. I'm going to check on the others."

The thoughts of Ruby refusing to eat and deliberately starving herself plague me all day. This child, whose life I wrestled to save, now refuses nourishment. I go next door to Auntie Ama to make sure all of the toddlers are healthy and to ask her advice about Ruby.

Mina is there. She comes each day to help Auntie Ama with the children. They love to crawl in her lap, and though blind, she expertly guides the daily gruel into the mouths of the little ones.

The next day when I visit Flora, Mina is there. Flora excitedly meets me at the door. "Sis

Pearl, oh Sis Pearl. Our prayers bin answered. Mina come las' night and hold 'n talk to dat baby all night. I beg her to lie down, but, no, she sit up and rock dat chile. Dis mornin' dat baby want all de bres'."

I am nearly bowled over by her enthusiasm and definitely overwhelmed by the news. Mina rocks the sleeping and satisfied Ruby. I am overjoyed that Ruby will live but uneasy that it took Mina's presence to keep the child alive. Five more days, if Ruby lives, she will get her name officially, and the quarters will welcome her. Thanks to Mina, not me.

She Ain't Like Udder Chillen

For those first months after Ruby was born, a frustrated Auntie Ama complains to me. "She ain't like my udder chillen. Don' wanta eat much, to be pick up at all, jus like to be to herself. She jus in her own worl."

I reassure the old woman who has never dealt with a baby as fussy as Ruby.

"She will be fine, just needs to adjust."

"So you say," grunts Auntie Ama.

But today, a year later, I ease into the suffocating, warm and raucous room of Auntie Ama's cabin. The putrid smell of asafetida worn on dirty strings by every child in the room permeates the air. I cover my nose. Pre–adolescent girls help Auntie Ama take care of the children whose mothers work in the fields during the day, have died, or have been sold away. The room is filled with little boys and girls wearing long shirts made of osnaburg, the fabric we're given for them, just an unbleached linen–hemp. All of the children are barefoot. Some scoot along the floor, others play in small groups in the corners of the room. Priscilla and Sarah are holding the babies while Lizzie dips steaming hot pot liquor into wooden bowls and adds a handful of crushed cornbread to each one. 1 look about the room, searching for Ruby, who I spot playing with two other children in the corner.

"Hello, my little Ruby, how are you today?" Ruby smiles as she reaches for me. I pick her up, hug her tightly, her face a full smile. Lizzie points to an empty chair where I sit with the now one-year-old Ruby on my lap. "I'll feed Ruby," I say as I gesture to Lizzie to bring a bowl of the pot liquor. "This looks good, little Ruby. I bet you enjoy this." Ruby smiles a big smile with two bottom teeth now showing. I take a spoon of the liquid dish, blow it gently, and spoon it into the waiting child's mouth. I smile to myself as I feed the hungry girl who once I feared would starve herself to death.

Auntie Ama comes over to the gustily eating Ruby and remarks, "Nebber knowed I'd see dis day. Dis chile eat up sumtin' now. Not like she use to be. In all my years bringin' up chillen I ain't nebber seen none like dis one."

Each day the Mistress comes to the cabin to be sure that the children are being fed enough and are healthy. "Y'all take care of our children," she comments with a smile as she leaves the cabin.

Auntie Ama rolls her eyes and sucks her teeth when Miss Charlotte leaves. "Dat 'oman don't care nuttin' 'bout dese here chillen. Jus' want to make sure dey able to work in de fields and bring a good price when dey sol at auction."

I hold my head down and feel uneasy as I absorb Auntie Ama's comment, even though I've heard it a hundred times. I don't respond but remember what Granny Abena was told by the coachman when she was first brought to the plantation. "You be alright if you keeps the nigga's healthy so they don't miss no work in the fields, and them babies nice and plump so that they bring a good price."

Ruby Is Missing

It has been five years since Ruby's tumultuous birth and her days of refusing to eat. Now she is a wide-eyed, curious, and strong-willed girl that I sense is not going to fit easily into the role of slave; something deep within Ruby seems to rebel against everything expected of her. I worry that the day will come when young Ruby will have to face reality. And that day comes soon enough.

It is a beautiful late fall Saturday afternoon. The sun is setting and the scrumptious aroma of rabbit and squirrel stews fill the air. The squeals of happy children play across the background of our lives as they scamper through the red and orange leaves piled around the big oak tree. The playing comes to a halt as the women line the children up for supper.

"Come on chillen," shouts Sally. "It time to eat!"

They gather around the big black pot, bowls in hand. I notice that Ruby is not in the mass of children. Worried, I rush over to them. "Where is Ruby? Have you seen Ruby? Was Ruby playing with you? Did you leave her somewhere?"

The children answer no to every inquiry. Finally Joe speaks up. "Ruby like to slip away and be by herself in the woods. I see her sometime. She prob'y out dere playin'."

"Ruby is missing; we have got to find her," I scream. The chatter and laughter of the throng halts, and two men volunteer to go with me to find Ruby. They tell the others, "Y'all stay here, we find her." Auntie Ama, a large woman, insists on coming as well. "Here I come, don't y'all dare leave me." She rolls along as fast as she can.

The search party heads out to the woods that edge the cotton fields. I try to keep Aunt Ama up with the men who stride ahead. I am panting and tears flow down my cheeks. Aunt Ama trudges uncomfortably behind me. Just as the two of us enter the woods, one of the men yells, "See her!"

"Here she is!" the other shouts. "We found her, she right here; she ain't hurt or nothing, she fine."

My heart skips a beat, and joy replaces my sense of uncertainty and terror. I hurry to Ruby, who sits along with Mina encircled by wild flowers. She plays with the long blades of grass. A warm smile covers Mina's face.

"Let me comb your hair, be still, stop moving so much," Ruby says to an imaginary friend. I am both relieved and amazed by the contented look that envelopes the often sullen face. But I am angered to see Mina sitting here with her. I believe that somehow she has encouraged this willful act.

"Honey, you can't just go off by yourself without telling anyone. The whole quarters is worried about you."

"But I'm not alone, I'm with Auntie Mina," insists Ruby. Mina sits with a smug smile stretching across her toothless gums.

"Not de chile fault. I come 'long wid her. I want to smell de flowers, feel de sunshine on dis ol' wrinkle face. Chile jus' pleasin' a ol' womin. Don' be mad at her." I feel my face reddening and my lips pursing. *I should have guessed you were behind this,* I think. *And I'm not mad at her, I'm mad at you!* But I say nothing. Auntie Ama who has equal status as an elder could pursue the matter with Mina, but she doesn't.

"So what are you doing here, Ruby?" I say ignoring Mina.

"Just playing, combing doll hair with the grass. See what I did?" She holds up for me the braided blades of grass.

37

"You gon git yor li'l fast self in a heap a trouble," warns the irritated Auntie Ama.

"This is where I like to be. It's fun here. This is where I like to come to "keep myself." Mina nods approval, sitting with arms folded, watching the encounter.

"Keep yourself?" I question.

Ruby nods yes. "So why can't I come to the woods to keep myself?"she asks.

"Dere she go agin' wit' dem questions, always why?" replies Auntie Ama. "You hab to stay where you spose to, dat's why. You got to do what you tol'."

"What's a slave?" inquires Ruby, feigning innocence. I look at Mina, knowing she is encouraging Ruby to question her status.

"You know what a slave is, "snorts Auntie Ama. "Somebody belong to somebody else, dey property, like dey own a cow or pig, dey own you."

"How are they going to own me? I'm not a cow," Ruby says stubbornly.

"But you a nigga and you is own by Massa Bellamy," declares a defiant Auntie Ama.

I smile to myself as I see the look that crosses Ruby's face and can only imagine the wheels turning in her little head. With a mischievous twinkle in her eyes, she toys with the idea of ownership. "My doll belongs to me? This dress belongs to me?" she asks pointing to her dress. "Who does our cabin belong to?"

"Massa Bellamy," replies Auntie Ama. But the questions don't stop and Ruby now has the opportunity to ask everything that's been forming in her mind since birth, it seems.

"Why do the women have to leave their babies with us and Auntie Ama to keep? Why does everybody work so hard? Why are the mothers so tired when they come to pick up the babies? Why is everybody scared of Percy?"

The answer is always the same. "Because they belong to Massa Bellamy." An exasperated look crosses Ruby's face, and I sense that she has already made up her mind that enslaved or not she belongs to no one. I steal a glance at Mina whose satisfied look betrays her part in this development.

The search group marches back to the gathering, all eyes upon Ruby as she is handed her gourd to get the stew. Sally comments, "Y'all 'member when dat chil' was born? She trouble 'den and she gon' keep bein' trouble, y'all jus' watch." The women laugh and shake their heads in amusement. Sally's prediction makes me recall

Auntie Ama's words when Ruby was only one year old.

Since her birth, I have honored her mother's request that I watch out for her. I make it a practice to spend time with the child. We have formed a peculiar relationship, a little like big and little sister, partly out of my guilt, and also my curiosity about the child who resisted being born. We are the two female slaves in the quarters that possess 'jewel' names; me Pearl, and Ruby, each of us born to a mother who survived only long enough after our births to glimpse our beauty and give us a distinctive name. To them, we were the most precious people in their brief lives. Our names made us special despite the conditions of our births and the lives that we would face as females in bondage.

I smile to myself as I watch Ruby happily sitting alone under the tree eating her supper. She is now five years old, long skinny legs, skin as smooth and shiny as maple syrup, deep brown eyes, so dark they appear black, and a thick head of hair, worn in a dozen plaits that cover her head.

I know Auntie Ama is right. Ruby is different. I have been secretly teaching her to read; now I question my decision. She is rebellious. I worry she will unconsciously flaunt her skill in front of whites, be whipped for impudence, run away one day, or worse yet, be sold. It never leaves my mind that Ruby resisted with all of her little might being born into slavery. I wonder if she, like her tribal Ibo ancestors, who committed suicide rather than face enslavement will choose one day to abandon this brutal life in any fashion she can. I also fear the influence that the old woman Mina has upon her.

Learning to be a Slave

Concealed, I watch Miss Charlotte walk down the rugged path forming the quarter's street and move quietly into each cabin while its inhabitants labor in the fields. She expects tidy cabins from women who labor from sunrise to sundown. I hold my breath, hoping that Miss Charlotte will find no pilfered food. I watch and wait as she weaves in and out.

As she nears, l slip next door to warn Auntie Ama that the Mistress will soon arrive. Miss Charlotte comes almost daily to Auntie Ama's cabin to see how well the young enslaved children are faring, and someone always calls out the warning. Miss Charlotte recoils and twitches her nose as she gets a whiff of the sacks worn by the children.

"Does this horrific-smelling medicine you douse these sacks with really help keep them healthy?" asks Miss Charlotte for the hundredth time.

"Sho do, Miss Charlotte," answers Auntie Ama.

Today, Miss Charlotte is choosing four of the older children she feels will be best suited to work in the Big House. Preparation for their role as house servants begins with Bible classes and being playmates of her children, Bo and Betsy. Ruby, now eight years old, is chosen along with Toby, Sanko, and Emily. My stomach sinks. This role for youngsters in the Big House comes as more of a burden than a blessing. My first inclination is to make some excuse for Ruby being unfit, but Miss Charlotte will question my not knowing my place. I worry that Ruby's willfulness will get her into serious trouble, even get her sold to another plantation.

As soon as Miss Charlotte departs, Auntie Ama and I begin to talk to Ruby about the proper way in which she is to behave in Miss Charlotte's presence. All of the quarters' children at some point begin to receive this kind of constant training in how to interact with whites. It doesn't really take them long to get it, but the adults consider learning how to act the part of a slave the most important lesson the children must take to heart.

"Ruby, you have been chosen to do something only a few of the children get to do," I say, attempting to flatter her. "You get to go to the Big House to learn Bible stories and to play with the Mistress's children. How special you are."

"You be good, you hear? None a yor questions. Jus' listen to Miss Charlotte, smile, and say thank you fo ebberting, includin' when it time to leave," warns Auntie Ama.

"Yes, Ma'am," Ruby says between tightly clenched teeth.

"Ruby darling, you are the smartest girl on Bellamy Plantation. I know you will know how to act," I say, hoping she does not pick up on the dread in my heart.

The next afternoon, Ruby goes up to the Big House with her friends. Miss Charlotte sets a table of lemonade and biscuits. She sees that Ruby is quite bright, and because of this, the Mistress enjoys having her in the Bible study group. She reads the children stories about the creation, Noah and the ark, and Jesus.

Trouble brews weeks later, however, when Miss Charlotte tells the children the story of Ham and how all of his descendants -- the people of Africa -- will have to be slaves for the rest of their lives, and how God wants them to obey their earthly masters. I can imagine Ruby rolling her eyes and twisting her mouth. *That can't be so,* she would think. Thankfully, she has been schooled enough by Auntie Ama and me not to ask questions, but she is mightily tempted. When it's time for lemonade and biscuits, she is divided in her thinking because she doesn't want to dispute anything the Mistress says, but the idea of God wanting black people to be enslaved is like a hot coal burning in her belly. She puts her mouth close to Toby's ear and makes him ask, "Why that so, Ma'am?"

"Why is what so Toby?" a surprised Miss Charlotte asks.

"Why God want us in the quarters to be slaves?" innocently asks Toby.

Miss Charlotte's eyes widen, her voice rises and her once smiling face is transformed as she glares at the young boy." Just because it is, because the Bible says so. Now, don't you question me, Toby. Don't you question a white person ever," she shouts as she gives Toby a vigorous smack across the head. Startled and contrite Ruby lowers her head, ashamed to look at Toby.

Toby is not invited back the next day, or ever, to join the Bible study and play group. Ruby is beginning to understand what it means to be a slave.

Just when l feel that Ruby is settling in, another problem arises. Bo, not able to hide in Hide 'n Seek without getting detected immediately, and pouting because of it, decides that it will be more fun to play master and slave. He demands that Sanko get on his knees and be a horse that he can ride. And Ruby and Emily have to fetch grapes from the arbor for Betsy and him. Incensed, Ruby gathers the grapes.

When she returns to the cabin, she has plenty of questions for Auntie Ama. "Why does he want to boss me? He says I've got to mind him. He's a stupid boy," complains Ruby.

"Oh, Ruby, honey, hush your mouth. Don't you ever say nothin' like that agin," warns Auntie Ama. "That kinda talk get you whip half to def'."

"What did I say so bad Auntie? It's true, he's a stupid boy. He doesn't know where to hide so he doesn't get caught. Hides in the same place every time. I'm smarter than him and you know it!" Before she knows what hit her, Ruby feels the sting of Auntie's slap across her face. The blow leaves Ruby reeling and hurt. Auntie has never laid a hand on her. A torrent of bitter tears pours from her eyes, not so much from the pain of the slap but the confusion as to why it happened. Ruby runs out to my cabin seeking solace. That night, however, Ruby learns the role she will have to play for the rest of her natural born days.

l grab Ruby and hold her tightly to my breast. "I am so sorry, Ruby. I wish I could tell you something that would turn all of this into make-believe, but I can't, "I say with contrition. "Auntie Ama's slap was not meant to hurt you but to protect you." A sad-eyed and somber Ruby listens.

With tear-filled eyes, a breaking heart, and a slow, sad voice, I reveal to Ruby the reality of her life. "Ruby, dear, even though it is not so, you are expected to act as though you are not as good as whites and that you are less smart. I know how smart you are, and you are smarter than Bo, but you can't act like it or voice it. You must always show that you understand your status as a slave with a bowed head, a closed mouth, and a smile," I explain. "You do not have to give up yourself, the beautiful Ruby that you are, but Auntie Ama is right: you can't act as though you are free when you are around whites. Do you understand?" Ruby nods her bowed head as tears trickle down her cheeks. "Everyone in the quarters has to learn this lesson," I add. "Watch and listen to adults in the quarters and you will learn what to do."

I look at this innocent child, my little Ruby, and my thoughts go back to the fateful night that I fought to bring her into this mean and brutal world of slave and master. Ruby forces the first tiny crack in the world within the confines of bondage that I have accepted for myself.

A still defiant Ruby proclaims, "Well I'm not going to play with Bo anymore. I'll be sick every time Miss Charlotte calls us to play." And she is. When the Mistress calls the children from the quarters, Ruby vomits her midday meal. I make excuses about the "poor little frail Ruby" and finally Miss Charlotte stops calling her to play.

This suits Ruby perfectly, I think. She delights herself creating dolls from tall grass, making mud pies, and talking to imaginary playmates, none of whom require her submission. She talks to butterflies and makes a pet of a terrapin that lives behind my cabin. When she is alone with the flowers, trees, and animals, she feels free, like she is "keeping herself."

About a month later, Auntie Ama and I decide we must give young Ruby chores to protect her. "Now, Ruby," says Auntie Ama, "if you are not gonna play with de udder chillen, I am gon hav to gib you some work to do. Mistress be real mad if she tink you ain't really sick and just don' wanna play wid Bo and Betsy," says Auntie Ama.

"Suits me, I rather work than play slave, "she replies.

"Shut yor mouth, girl. I don tol' you 'bout dat mout a yors. One a dese days you gon see what a smart mout gits a nigga."

And sooner than later she does.

This incident helps to determine how Ruby will chisel her freedom silently and without calling attention to herself. Auntie Ama takes Ruby to watch as Roy, Hannah's fifteen-year-old son, gets some stripes from the overseer. He has stolen a chicken. Roy suggests to the overseer that since he is enslaved, he has already worked for the chicken. For his insubordination of both stealing and being mouthy, the entire quarters is forced to watch him receive fifty stripes. The lashings are public spectacles intended to instill fear in us and discourage any outward sign of dissatisfaction with our lot. Roy's shirt is torn off and he is forced face down on the ground. Three stakes form a triangle. Roy's arms are tied to two of them, and his legs are pulled tight together and his feet tied to the third stake. The stripes are not inflicted by the overseer but by Sam the black driver. This is the first time Ruby has taken notice of Sam, although she has heard his name cursed by most of those who live in the quarters.

Sam spits, leans back with a look of arrogance combined with hatred and proceeds to unmercifully whip Roy almost to death. Roy moans and tries to twist his body but will not cry out. It seems that Sam puts more effort into each lick to make Roy scream, but he refuses.

Tears stream down Ruby's face at the horror. She is repulsed by Roy's bloody, torn back, and the wicked pleasure Sam derives from administering the blows. She quietly slips to the back of the crowd and runs to the cabin. She sobs until she feels that her body is an empty shell. The image of Sam, smugly raising his arm and putting all of his might into each whip of the lash lingers in her mind. She comes to hate Sam as much as she hates slavery. From this day forward, her stomach turns at the sight of him.

Roy is picked up by the men and brought to the sick house where Pearl and the women administer to his back so badly beaten that bones show and flesh falls away. Ruby stands silently at the door, watches, and listens.

"That boy don' never learn ta keep his mout shut," cries his mother Hannah. "Yeh got to just keep yor head down and say yessir. Ain't in no way right but dat da way fo us niggas. Keep yor head down and mout shut."

It is during Roy's recuperation that Ruby starts to avail herself of my invitations to help me in the sick house. While children her age carry wood and do other chores on the plantation, Ruby helps me. I hear a great deal between the two of them.

"This what you get for talkin' back to white folks," Roy says to Ruby.

Ruby shakes her head and asks him, "Why do we have to be slaves anyway?"

Ah ain't gon be one long," replies Roy. "When Ah'm well, Ah'm leaving, Ah gots to be free."

"Take me with you, please," begs Ruby.

"You too little now, but when you git older, you kin leave. 'Til den, just git yor freedom in de li'l ways dat you make. Slip away to de woods, "advises Roy. "Steal you what you want to eat, you work for it. If you want to run, cain't have no chillen. When you git yor flowers keep to yor'self, stay away from all de men in de quarters, or you will hab a baby."

I watch Ruby listening in amazement and wondering what it means to "get your flowers." I want to tell him to quit talking to her but I know they would just talk when I was absent. At least this way I get to hear what he's putting in her head.

Roy continues. "Cain't see yor'self as no slave, gotta say to yor'self, dat means dem, don' mean me. Got to be slick, grin and smile 'n when you can, got to snatch little bits a freedom here and dere. Got to own yor freedom in yor head 'til y'all kin run."

"I have dreams," Ruby answers. "In my dreams, I am in a different place. I'm not a slave. I wasn't ever meant to be a slave. God didn't mean for me to be born a slave."

"Just 'member to keep yor freedom in yor own head and don't have no slave baby," Roy reinforces.

It takes almost three months for Roy to heal but when he does, we all hear that he and four other boys ran away to a place called Florida. Ruby cries, knowing that her friend has left her and will be free. But I fear that the words he told her -- "*Keep your freedom in your head and don't have no slave baby*" will stay in her mind forever.

The Flowers

At age twelve, Ruby is assigned to the "trash gang," a group of girls her age who work on the plantation grounds pulling weeds and hoeing. She seems to like the company of her friends but is happy to be chosen to bring water to the workers in the fields. I know how Ruby treasures the freedom she feels when she is alone. She is always seeking that "little bit of freedom" that Roy talked about.

I watch her look out at the blanket of cotton plants over which weary black bodies stoop in the scorching sun and see her face get sad. How long will it be before she has to join those miserable souls?

She's brought back to earth when the overseer waves her to bring water to the workers. She grabs the heavy bucket and starts down the rows of women. She dips the gourd into the bucket and each worker takes a big gulp of water. Her heart sinks as she looks into the sad eyes of the barely dressed woman whose calloused and pricked hands reach for the gourd. She finishes the row and is going back to get another bucket when she senses wetness in her underwear.

Ruby kneels in the tall grass near the field where the women go to do their business. She pulls down her underwear. Inside, a circle of blood. She grabs the buckets and scurries through the field and back to the quarters. She races into the sick house, breathing hard and sweating profusely.

"Sista Pearl, Sista Pearl," she shouts. "Oh, my God! I am dying! Dying before I ever get to be free!"

"Be quiet, girl, don't you see these sick people in here?" I ask. "Whatever it is, it can wait until I finish here."

"But it can't wait, Sista Pearl. I got to talk to you right now, "insists Ruby.

"Now, girl, you get on out of here. These people are sick and I don't have time for talking," I say.

"But I'm sick, too," answers Ruby.

I roll my eyes up to the heavens and motion for Ruby to follow me. "Okay, come over here and let me see." I take Ruby behind a screen and wait as she pulls her pants down. "You're not sick, my child, you finally got your flowers." I laugh but with rue. *Now it begins*, I think.

"My flowers?" Ruby's eyes are wide and her mouth drops open. "What do I do now, Pearl?" asks an excited and confused Ruby.

I go to a box, take out a piece of cloth and give it to Ruby. "Put this in your underwear like this until I finish this evening." I fold the cloth and show Ruby how to place it.

Then I ask, "But Ruby, where are you supposed to be?"

"I just stopped by on my way to get water for the hands," says Ruby.

"Well, you better hurry back before that mean old Percy thinks you are gone too long," I caution.

"See you later, Pearl, and thank you, "says Ruby, pausing on her way out. "So this is what it means to get your flowers." She does not smile, and I think of her old friend Roy and what he told her from his sickbed.

After finishing dinner and their evening chores, a dozen or more women gather in my small cabin. They sit in a circle on cloths laid upon the earthen floor. Six girls are invited to sit inside the circle, my Ruby one of them. Candles placed on the table and around the room highlight the sad and worried expressions on the women's faces, and the inquisitive and anxious looks of the girls who are going to be told about this significant event in their lives. They notice the looks on the women's faces.

"Did we do somethin' wrong?" asks one of the girls. "Why dey look so sad?" asks another. I know the thoughts in Ruby's head must be crashing into each other. I think again that she must be remembering Roy's warning from four years ago -- "*When you get your flowers you can have a baby, and if you have a baby, it is harder to run away.*" She probably thinks that now she's got her flowers she'll have a baby?

What the girls soon hear is that this ritual will teach them the reality of being a female slave. They will learn that they are not only required to produce for the master through their labor but that their womanhood will be used to reproduce more slaves for his profit as well.

Ruby notices my discomfort. I always hate these talks. I feel at odds with the old blind Mina who talks about the African ways. I suspect that Mina might use some of her knowledge to help the girls not to have babies. But my concern and my job is that the girls learn how to take care of themselves and if they became pregnant to have a healthy child. I give way to the old woman because she is an elder. She is also known as a conjure woman, something that Granny Abena, a Christian, warned me about.

Mina, small, very dark and wiry, with a pushed-up nose and fierce unseeing eyes pulls her chair closer to the girls. She wears a head rag. Mina is seldom seen without the corn cob pipe in the corner of her mouth. Folks in the quarters say she can out-cuss any man.

The girls lean forward, intrigued by Mina and curious about this new womanhood. I feel slightly jealous of the attention they -- especially Ruby-- give to Mina.

"You girls is wimmins now," she begins. "We welcome you to the circle of de wimmin on dis here plantation. De wimmin, she hab a pow'rful job bringin' up de chillen. Becomin' a wimmin, dat a good ting on de one han' and not so good on de udder on dis here plantation. It a good ting when you find a good man who luv you and you and he hab a beautiful baby."

Sally interrupts Mina. "Get to it, Auntie Mina. Tell dem girls like it is."

"Well," continues Mina, "now dat you got yor flowers, kin have a baby. A baby nice 'n all but you mus' be ver careful. Now dat old overseer Percy be lookin' at you all de time. He be wantin' to gib you some little something to make you like him, but if you git alone wid him, he hurt you bad and soon

59

you have a baby. You may jus' be a girl still in yor head. Den after you hab dat baby, dey sell it quick, cause dem yellow babies bring top dolla, 'n you grow up 'n be sad de res a yor life."

As Mina talks, I feel Ruby look at me, watching. I am looking into the faces of the girls and seeing the joy of childhood drain away and the fright of a slave girl's purpose fall heavily like a millstone on their backs. Ruby lowers her head as tears fill her eyes. What Roy said to Ruby was truth; these flowers are not such a good thing after all.

Hannah speaks next. "I dun had all but tree of my six livin' chillen sol' away from me. Some belong to my George, but sometimes dat old Percy come in my cabin and steal me out at night. Ain't nuttin' George can do. I hate dat Percy, I hate ebby ting 'bout his lowdown ass. But when I holds dat baby in my arm, and breathe in dat little sweet baby smell, and holds it to my bosom, I starts to love it. Love it like a mudder does, but den once I start to love it, dey takes it away. I jus don' made some money for de Massa.

"So why we hab you girls here tonight cause we wants to help you much as we can. Take dis cloth." Hannah passes a strip of muslin to each girl. "Tie your breasts down so you won't be showin' soon. Den try not to complain 'bout no women's trouble if you can help it. Less folk know, de better."

"Stay clear a Percy. Keep yor head down and dont look at dat man. Keep as far away from him as you can. Whatever you do, don' let him trick you into his cabin."

"And not only Percy do you have to worry about," says Flora. "Sometime, frens a Massa Ben come down to de quarters wantin' a black gal. Got to be careful of dem, too."

One of the girls, frightened and shaking, raises her hand. "So how we protec ourself?"

"Good question, we comin to dat right now. You gon hear some tales 'bout what to do." One by one the women stand and tell their stories.

Sadie, a tall heavy-set woman, begins. "Dat old Percy de oberseer come up behin' me, touchin' my breasts and all. I turns around and ask that buckra what he wants wid me. He say it my time. I say I ain't gots no time for you. I gots me a good man. Ain't nuthin' yor scrawny ass kin do fo me. He turns real red in de face and rears back and try to trow me down. Well, we tussles and rolls all ober de floor. I dig my fingernails in his face and scratch him up real bad. He yell he gon kill me, but he jus' back away when I walk out de door. I still livin' and I ain't

61

nebber had no more trouble outta him." The women and girls cheer, clap, and laugh for Sadie, who smiles shyly and ducks her head.

Mary Jane, a tall, thin-boned woman with teeth that seem too large for her face is next. "Well, I ain't as strong as Sadie, but when old Percy come up, he pull me real close to him. I smell dat bad breath, make me sick. I say to myself, dis is not de day to mess wid dis here nigga gal. He start putting his old smelly lips on me. I turn and sink my teef in de top of his ear. He scream and try to shake me off but dese old teef jus keep hangin' on. Den I run from de cabin spittin' 'n cryin'. Tink I bit off a piece a his ear, but serve him right."

As five or six women tell their stories, the women and girls cheer for all the braveness among themselves. The girls look up at them with respect and admiration.

Then Mina again. "You cain't be scareda the lash. Yeah, it sho do hurt but you got to protec yor'self. Whatebber you do, don't let ol' Percy or any white man trick you into a cabin, the laundry room, the barn or anywhere where dey can rape you. You hear me?" The girls nod, looking at one another in fear.

"Now, Massa gon soon try to match you up wid a man, he don't care what man or if you like de man or not. Jus want you to go wid dat man so you kin start habbin' babies for Massa to sell. Bes' ting to find yor own sweetheart, somebody you tink you would like to jump de broom wid. Don' mean Percy won't come after you, but at lese you like de fadder a yor chillen."

Sarah, a young woman with big smiling brown eyes who recently jumped the broom with her sweetheart Peter, is next. "Once you get yor flowers, your body gon start changin'. Yor tits gon grow and you gon start to feel diffrent. You gon start to like de boys. Like Auntie Mina say, once you see a boy who you fancy, start to talk to him. If ya'll like each other go 'head and jump de broom. It sho feel good to snuggle up wid someone you love."

The women laugh and tease Sarah about being a new bride. "You jus wait, we see what you be sayin' in a while after dat man don 'bout wore you out."

I watch Ruby as determination sets into her brow. Her lips purse, jaws puff, and her eyes burn with anger. *Now she knows why I didn't want to tell her about the flowers long ago. I couldn't spoil her childhood world. Once again she learns even more about what it means to be a slave.*

Ruby raises her hand to be recognized. Mina acknowledges her. "Is Percy the father of all these yellow children in the quarters?" Ruby asks.

"Well, we need to warn you 'bout somebody else," says Mina. "Sam de driver like to take his pleasure wid de women in de quarters, too. 'Specially de younguns like you. Watch out for him. Old Sam has a few chillen here in de quarters. Dey usually get put in de Big House cuz dey part white seein's how Sam be the Mass's chile."

There is a slight pause, as some women look down and others look at me.

"We wimmin try to avoid dat Sam as much as we can. Cain't stand him eidder. He a white man's nigga, do everything Massa tell him to," adds Susie.

"You know why that so, don't you?" Susie continues." Sam dat old man William Bellamy's gran-chile. Massa and him be cousins. Old Massa William hab two boys, Richard, Sam's papa, 'n Felix, Ben's pa. Both Old Massa William's sons die young, first Richard, den Felix. Make our Massa Ben in charge. But dat old Miss Emily still kickin', she 'bout de bes' one ob dem all. Like her a heap bedder dan dat Miss Charlotte marry to Massa Ben."

64

"Yeh, most of Massa's sistahs and brudders git de bes jobs on de plantation. Dey don't work in de fiels like de res of us black niggas," says Hannah, glancing at me out of the side of her eyes.

"Try not to cross Sam. He kin make a nigga's life miserble," chimes Daisy. "Yeh, like he did Neeny. She don' want him but he want her. Make her have all dem chillen. But her chillen all up in de big house now. Dey kin eben slip her some biscuits once 'n a while prob'ly nebber git sol' south."

I watch Ruby wince each time the women mention the man that both men and women in the quarters hate. Sam's name has filled her with dread ever since she saw him whip Roy. She can barely stand their speaking the terrible man's name. *Will I ever tell her that he and I are related? I fear for when she learns it.*

"Y'all jus gots ta be extra careful now dat dem flowers don come. It ain't no way easy for a woman in dis here life," warns Mina.

I watch Ruby reflect upon these words, and my heart sinks. Her face has taken on a stubborn, hard look, and it's as if I can hear her brain working: she will do anything she has to do never to have a baby; she will "keep" herself, as she calls it. I see it as clear as if she's talking out loud.

65

That night, I decide to have Ruby become my permanent assistant in the sick house and to apprentice her as a midwife.

The Sick House

Ruby is a great help to me. She is good with the patients, excellent at root and herb gathering, and she reads so well she can decipher Dr. Smith's notes about the patients that he sees. She has planted an herb garden in the back of the sick house filled with mint, rosemary, tansy, sage, mullein, and catnip that she's dug up in the woods and the lavender meadow. My plan that one day she will take my place as the midwife for the quarters seems to fit with her.

Ruby can instinctively detect rebellion masked as illness. She and Sancho joke about his constant stays in the sick house. "Ruby, I be sick any time de sick spirit hit me, jus' cain't help it," says Sancho. Ruby falls into uproarious laughter and encourages him. "You are always welcome, Sancho, and I'll take good care of you."

When Miss Charlotte stops by to check on the patients, Ruby acts as though they are sicker than they are. "Miss Charlotte, I am worried about Sancho," she says. "I just don't know if he should go back to work in the fields so soon. It just might kill him, and Master will lose a valuable slave." When Miss Charlotte is out of earshot, Ruby and the patients have a big laugh. I enjoy seeing her happy and playful, so I really never scold her collusion with the slaves who fake illnesses.

Ruby often recoils, however, at sight of the tired and broken bodies that come into the sick house. "They are being worked to death," she says with her now always vigilant take on the Bellamys. But it is flapping skin and exposed bone from the backs of those lashed that send her into rages. Unlike me, she is not able to simply try to comfort and heal the poor broken souls. There is nothing about enslavement that Ruby accepts or can adapt to.

As much as she seems to like the sick room work, it is the Bible stories she tells to the sick of places far from the plantation that eventually start to provoke questions within her about slavery and the differences between the whites and the slaves. The plantation consists of the quarters, the fields, the Big House and the woods beyond. She believes that anyone with any sense at all would know that the world cannot be this small. If God created the world, all of it surely did not fit into this small space, as large as the plantation appears to be. Ruby goes off on this tack and begins to yearn to know more about the world that God created.

This, too, will end badly.

As soon as Ruby turns fourteen, she devises a plan. She tells me that she thinks to herself, "If I can work in the Big House, I can hear more about the world. I know that the Master and Mistress travel far." I ignore her, but later she says, "Sista Pearl, I want to work in the Big House. Please talk to Miss Charlotte and encourage her to let me work there," she demands.

"Ruby, you don't have the disposition to work in the Big House. You will hate it. They may wear better clothes than you and eat better food, but working in the Big House isn't as good as you think it is," I caution.

"I'm smart, I can do the work. I promise not to let my mind wander and I know how to keep my lips tight and my head down. Please, Sista Pearl, I need to be in the Big House," she pleads.

"I have never heard you talk like this before. I thought you liked helping the sick and having the freedom to go into the woods to gather herbs. And remember how you hated being up there when you were little?"

"Well, to tell you the truth, I'm older now and I think if I work in the Big House, I can hear things that will let me know about the world that

God created. I think I can learn new things. And Mistress likes me."

"Oh, my sweet dear Ruby, do you promise to be good?"

"I promise, Sista Pearl, I'll be the best house nigga they got." She grins at me, but I cannot smile back.

Against my discomfort with the idea, I petition Miss Charlotte on Ruby's behalf. On my recommendation, the Mistress invites Ruby to come to work in the Big House as a servant.

The Big House

At first, the Big House is fascinating to Ruby. Now that she is older, she is more aware and at first becomes taken with the expansive rooms, the polished furniture and portraits of women with beautiful clothing. But it doesn't take long for her to become increasingly disenchanted with serving the white masters and their children. She has to work hard. She isn't learning much about the wider world. She misses us in the quarters.

"It is not what I imagined, Sista Pearl," she tells me. "I thought I would be learning about all the places the white folks visit and about the world outside of Bellamy plantation."

As I knew it would, her life has become more and more stifling to her. She must live in the special cabin for house servants near the Big House so they can always be available. She works all day peeling and chopping vegetables, waiting on the Bellamys, then cleaning up afterward. Most nights it is almost midnight when she gets to sleep.

"I miss living with you, Sista Pearl. And spending time at the sick house."

Friendly old Bertha the cook is the only house servant Ruby can tolerate. She finds the others haughty. "They talk and act like they're white, Sista. And they look down on field slaves, call them ignorant niggas. Don't they know they aren't any freer than the field hands?"

She wears Miss Charlotte's or Betsy's hand-me-down clothes and gets to share the leftovers with the other servants, but she tells me she feels it is harder to "keep" herself in the Big House. Ruby feels that the constant bowing, holding her head down, acting invisible, and just being around white folks all the time is stealing her integrity, her special sense of self.

Ruby says to me one day, "I feel like I am choking to death sometimes. Miss Charlotte is always standing over me, watching everything I do. Every time I turn around, here she comes again." She mimics Miss Charlotte. "'I think you missed a spot, Ruby. You better work a little faster, Ruby. It's almost time to set the table, Ruby.' Lord, I hate to see her coming." Ruby tells me she's always thinking things to herself like, *Why don't you try polishing silver all day, bitch?*

I scold her, tell her to think of the Lord or her lavender field. Ruby's jaw stiffens. "Miss

Charlotte stands next to me and watches me count every piece of silverware. What does she think a nigga is going to do with a silver spoon anyway? Can't buy freedom with it."

Miss Charlotte announces to the house slaves a big dinner party is coming up, more than twelve guests expected. Ruby does not look forward to it. "It's bad enough bowing and scraping for Massa and Missus, can't even get themselves a glass of water, Pearl. Now twelve more to wait on hand and foot." She scowls as she tells me how she has to stand rigid and erect for three hours or more while the white people ramble on about the most boring topics -- the price of cotton, who is not doing their duty on the patrol, or "those God-damned abolitionists."

I spend my days praying for my girl.

"And they have so much of everything, Pearl, it's sickening." It is late Sunday night and she has sneaked away to the quarters to talk to me. She has to tell me about the dinner party, she says, just to get it off her chest. "Everything is perfect and I made it that way, Sista Pearl. The mahogany gleams because I polished it. Pink flowers from the garden are perfect in silver vases because I picked them and fixed them. The silver candleholders march down the table and can't be an inch out of line. That china

73

she calls 'fine bone' is honest to God trimmed in silver and ringed with garlands of tiny pink roses. Crystal glasses and fancy carved silverware are perfect at every plate. They have such silly rules about things that don't matter. They have to use a dozen knives and forks and spoons apiece!" She is indignant. "I can only think of our wood spoons and our gourds."

She tells the whole evening: "At seven o'clock the guests are arriving. Each lady is on the arm of a gentleman; Master Ben and Miss Charlotte lead them in. Jacob the butler, who thinks he's so handsome in his livery and so proper in speech and manner, welcomes each of the guests and guides each one to assigned seats. He's good at bowing and scraping. He gives me his old chin-up movement that means I better stand erect, no leaning on the buffet or shifting from leg to leg. His prim signal is also supposed to remind me that I am to be as invisible as possible. This isn't too hard to do because to them I am just like a piece of furniture. I hate him, too." I sigh. The girl is growing into hate like she's growing into her woman's body. Why I let her become a house slave worries on me. Although I do know she wouldn't let it go until she got her way.

"So then, old Jacob, he nods his head at me," she continues, "and I have to bring a dish from the serving table. What I'm carrying smells so good I almost faint. My nostrils soak up that aroma of roasted quail bathed in a creamy sauce, and I hope the crowd won't be greedy and eat every morsel.

"I'm standing there, expressionless, my mind wandering, when I catch Thomas Andrews say, '…Negroes down south….'

"Now this man is one of the richest men in the area according to Jacob, who also tells me to watch his fine manners. Ugh."

"I'm all ears as this is a topic of concern to me. 'I hear that, too,' says Joe Smith. "A real market in Alabama and Louisiana. The house slaves tell me he's known to deal with slave trades in the area.'

"'Old Perkins made a killing last month,' adds William Morris, a red-faced man with a tuft of white hair. 'I sold a whole batch of yellow younguns to a trader. Even took the baby.' Can you believe he would say that?" She is indignant.

"Then Andrews talks again: 'Since they banned bringing Negroes in, breeding them is the only way to keep a good stock.'

"'What are you doing to keep your niggas reproducing?' asks Master Bellamy.

"Andrews is all puffed up with himself and says, 'Just read a great article. Got to encourage them to marry, start a family. Give them passes to visit other plantations to find a mate. Got to work out deals to split the profits if your wench has the baby outta my buck.'

"As I'm listening to this awful talk, Pearl, my heart races and I try to keep my lips from twitching. *Wait until I tell Pearl about this,* is what I'm thinking. And they keep talking.

"Mr. Smith says, 'How is it working?'

"Andrews says, 'Damn well for me, but only if I sweeten the pot a little.'

"Now Bellamy talks: 'How's that?'

"Andrews is off and running: 'Offer incentives to the wenches. If they get pregnant, I ease up on the work some, especially when they get close to time. Lose that labor in the fields but get my return. They like it too if you give the mother double rations. That way the niggas won't steal as much, either. And if the pickaninny lives to be a year old, I give the mother some cloth for a new dress. Gives them an incentive to take good care of that baby. You know how careless they can be with their babies.'

"It's all I can do not to scream, Sista. The more I'm around white people the more horrible I think they are.

"So then Mr. Morris bows his head and says sheepishly, 'But you know the real money comes from those with white blood.' The men smile to themselves but you should have seen the women. They couldn't look at each other, and they glared at the men. I thought my chest would burst."

She exhales as loudly as she can while I can almost see her mind racing.

"My thought was this, Sista, that I had to tell the women in the quarters that it's not enough to work us to death, they plan to breed us like horses."

"But, Ruby," I say. "Didn't you hear the women say this when we had the flowers ceremony?"

"Well, yes, but now it's a plan!" she says with vehemence. "Master Ben wants to make slave babies just to sell! It isn't right! What are we going to do?"

"Ruby, dear girl. I don't know." In my mind I know there's little we can do. "You get some sleep."

"Pearl! This is really important," says Ruby wringing her hands and rocking from side to side.

"Ruby, I promise we will talk. Now get to your cabin before you get into trouble."

She leaves crying, shoulders bowed. I cannot sleep. My mind drifts to Auntie Ama's and Granny Abena's words years ago.

The mistress had come to Auntie Ama's to be sure that the children were being fed enough and were healthy. "Y'all take care of our children," she commented with a smile as she left the cabin. Auntie Ama rolled her eyes and sucked her teeth, as usual when the mistress left. "Dat 'oman don't care nuttin 'bout dese here chillen. Jus' want to make sure dey able to work in de fields." I remember feeling uneasy as I absorbed Auntie Ama's comment. I didn't respond but recollected for the thousandth time what Granny Abena said she was told by the coachman when she was first brought to the plantation, the whole thing about "You be alright if you keeps the niggas healthy so they don't miss no work in the fields, and them babies nice and plump so that they bring a good price."

~~~~~~~~~~~~

By Sunday, the significance of Ruby's warning comes to us by way of the minister preaching to the quarters. Ruby looks annoyed as she stands back by the door and watches the other house servants take their seats behind the family on the veranda. I can just hear her talking to herself about how proud of themselves they are in their hand-me-down clothes walking behind the master and mistress to sit with the family, separate from the field slaves. And, really, she's right -- the women all prim with their mouths pursed and Jacob with his tight jaw, looking arrogant. From Ruby's opinion, and mine, too, nobody including the mistress can out-dress the women in the quarters when they step out on Sunday. She smiles proudly as she looks out onto the lawn at the beautifully adorned women she loves. I love her.

Producing babies for sale is certainly not considered a sin in the eyes of the minister. He bases his sermon on the first chapter of Genesis. "The God created great whales, and every living creature moveth, which the waters brought forth abundantly, after their kind, and every winged fowl after his kind and God saw that it was good. And God blessed them, saying be fruitful, and multiply, and fill the waters in the seas and let fowl multiply on the earth." He clears his throat, stands up straight and looks deeply into the eyes of the enslaved. "And God created Adam and Eve, and God blessed them, and God said unto them, be fruitful and multiply and replenish the earth." His voice rises and with a kind of forceful growl he says, "It is God's command that you multiply, reproduce, and replenish the earth.

This is not my will or your master's will but God's will. You must fill the earth with children."

Master Bellamy steps to the platform after the minister completes his sermon. "I know that sometimes it seems difficult to follow God's will. To help you do the will of God, as soon as you know that you are with child, let Pearl know and we will decrease your workload and increase your ration of food. Also, if you take good care of your child, I will give you cloth to make a new dress."

The women in the crowd exchange glances, some with puzzled looks on their faces. Most remember the great slave auction that took place at the Race Course in Savannah years before. They identify with the sadness and grief of broken families from another plantation when they were sold. The greatest fear among the enslaved on Bellamy Plantation is to have families torn apart by trades or sales.

Ruby fidgets with her collar and looks out with envy on the women in the quarters sitting on the lawn with friends and family. She waves a little hello to me, resentful that she will not be able to join the quarters after the sermon in having a picnic under the big oak tree. There will be chicken pilau, fried fish, stews and other delicious foods. We will spend the afternoon eating, visiting, and maybe singing and dancing. Only as dark falls will we go back to our cabins and prepare for the next day. Maybe only an afternoon, but the quarters get a snatch of freedom.

Tears fill Ruby's eyes as she and the other house servants disappear into the house to serve lunch, clean up, and then prepare for supper. Only late tonight will the house servants finish and return to their cabins. I know Ruby; she is feeling angry and more than a little jealous. Soon she will be plotting to get out of being a house slave. And sooner than she thinks, Ruby's time in the Big House will end in dramatic fashion.

The Poisonings

A scurrilous allegation sends a sedate small dinner party into pandemonium, Ruby tells me one Sunday night. Judge and Mrs. Danforth are supper guests. Mrs. Danforth is one of the Bellamy guests that Ruby likes least. She drops her shoulders as the Danforth's arrive.

"I say to myself, Sista Pearl, *Look at that prune-faced, fish-lipped bitch. Stuffed into that awful pink dress that is the same color as her pale skin. Can out-eat a horse. Bellamy's must save for a month to feed her.* She orders me around the whole time. Won't let Jacob help, says let the girl do it. I hate her."

Ruby has a way with words, I've learned. Her stories are like a play.

"Mrs. Danforth smiles and graciously greets Jacob but leers at me," Ruby says. "The gossip in the kitchen is that Mrs. Danforth dislikes and mistrusts all female slaves. Her husband has several half-white children on their plantation that are said to be the children of his mistress, the head house servant."

Ruby smiles, but it's not a nice smile; it's full of spite.

"...about to pick up the heavy tureen of oyster stew off the sideboard to give to Jacob when Mrs. Danforth starts rambling hysterically. I stand still, my back to the table, shocked at her words. 'My sister in Richmond wrote me,' Mrs. Danforth says, 'about friends of hers who were murdered by the nigga cook and house girls. The wenches poisoned them!' She practically screamed this out. I turn around to see heads fly up at the table, all staring at Mrs. Danforth.

"'What?'" screams Miss Charlotte.

"'The whole family, children and all, got sick after supper,' she says. 'Took to bed and died the next day. The whole family.' Mouths drop even farther and eyes widen as fear circles the table. Jacob stands like a stone. Me, too.

"Mrs. Dandforth isn't done, though. 'Put Jameson weed in their soup, damned niggas. Thieves and murderers all of them,' she shrieks. Her nostrils flare and spittle flies from her mouth.

"'Oh, my God,' cries Miss Charlotte.' That is just awful.'

"'My sister,' squeaks Mrs. Danforth, 'says niggas in Richmond have just gone mad, all this talk about secession from the Union making them crazy.' Mrs. Danforth's body is shaking, and then I start to shake as she says the next thing. 'Do you trust the wenches in your house Charlotte?'

"I am frightened now, but Miss Charlotte says, 'Please calm down, Alice. You are safe here. Of course I trust my servants. They are most faithful, they would never hurt us. Bertha has been cooking in this family for years, Jacob is just a fine servant, and I have known Ruby since she was a little girl, used to teach her the Bible.'

"Then Master Ben has to say something. 'Charlotte's right, Alice, calm down,' he says like he's the boss. 'Jacob, please brings Mrs. Danforth a whiskey.'

"'Yes, sir,' says old scaredy cat Jacob, who quickly disappears.

"I have turned back around now and am staring down at the tureen, suddenly imagining the mouthwatering stew full of cream and plump oysters. It is my favorite, and so I just go into my own world and come up with an idea. I have to say I surrendered to a temptation beaming in my mind. Listen to this."

I sigh deeply, uncertain as to what might come next from Ruby's mouth.

"When Mrs. Danforth is calmed down some, Miss Charlotte gestures to Jacob to serve the meal.

Jacob signals me to bring the stew. I bow my head, lower my eyes and inch stiffly toward the table, lips and chin trembling. My hands are shaking so uncontrollably that it appears I might drop the tureen. Jacob's head jerks up and he races to retrieve the dish from me. The Bellamys and Danforths give each other furtive glances. As I hoped, Mrs. Danforth's eyes widen, and terror blanches her salmony face. She gulps out loud and stammers to her hostess, 'Ch…Charlotte, frankly, I would feel more comfortable if you make the wench eat the soup first.'

"And Miss Charlotte pipes up with, 'Well, certainly, Alice, if this is what you want, but I can assure you the stew is fine. Ruby, go get a bowl and spoon.' I go to the kitchen house but linger until Jacob comes in hissing at me to get moving.

"Miss Charlotte looks at me funny and says, 'What took you so long, Ruby?'

"Nothing, Ma'am, had to find a clean one," I say.

"Old fishface practically yells, 'I tell you what's wrong; the niggas are trying to poison us! Fill up her bowl. Make her eat the whole thing!'

"I jerk back and I breathe hard and I say with huge innocence, 'Miss Charlotte, you want me to eat

86

the Master's and Missus's food? I can't do that, it for y'all.'

"A steely faced Miss Charlotte says in a firm voice, 'Eat the stew, Ruby.'

"I fill the bowl and slowly sip and savor tiny spoonfuls of oyster stew. I bite into a plump oyster and think, *This is soooo good. I just want to gobble it all up.* But I manage to eat it slowly and deliberately. After each bite, I give a pleading look at Miss Charlotte. Jacob watches with fear-filled eyes, and the diners hold their breaths as they watch a slave girl eat their stew. When the bowl is empty I show it to Miss Charlotte, but I keep my head down. *Can't look satisfied,* I think.

"And then for some reason, Jacob acts out of character and steps forth to say, 'See, Miss Charlotte, the food is fine. Bertha and Ruby would never harm you and Master Ben.'

"Then Master Ben chimes in. 'If the stew was poisoned Ruby would be withering in pain now. Look at her -- she is fine.'

"Satisfied that the stew is not poisoned, the Bellamys and the Danforths finally allow Jacob to refill and serve the dish. I take my position at the buffet, so full and content I can barely stay awake."

87

Ruby tells me that by the time she clears the table and returns to the kitchen house, Bertha and the other servants are doubled over in laughter. She told me that Bertha said, 'Gal, I thought you was gon be hung or sold, you too much.'

Ruby smiles slightly and is soon bubbling over with laughter. She can hardly contain herself. "Pearl, I had the best oyster stew tonight I'll ever have."

I don't say much, for I fear for her, as always. But I am secretly gleeful for my girl. The next day the poisoning story is all over the quarters. Folks start to call Ruby "Oyster." I pretend that I am not amused, and I do have to caution her. "Keep this up and you will soon be whipped." Ruby shrugs her shoulders.

The Nigga Disease

Each day Ruby's dislike for the Big House grows, and her litany of complaints gets longer: *Grown folks can't put on their clothes, pick up anything they drop. Can't comb their own hair. Get themselves a handkerchief. More like babies than grown.* Though she is desperate to leave, Ruby finds herself in a delicate situation. She asked me to intervene on her behalf to work in the Big House and pestered until I gave in. I remember one of many conversations. "Pearl, I want to work in the Big House. I am tired of totin' water to the fields. It's too hot out there and some days I feel like I will pass out. You are close to Master Ben and Miss Charlotte. Will you please get me work in the Big House?"

Miss Charlotte often comments to me about how good a servant Ruby has become, but after the oyster stew incident I worry that Ruby will do something the Bellamy's will find unforgivable and sell her.

Mistress Charlotte is not the only one who takes notice of Ruby. Ruby tells me that Bo, Mistress Charlotte's son, now sixteen years old, is home from school for the summer. He has grown tall and with his green eyes and wavy red hair, he is handsome. Bo is also ready to become a man by having himself some fun with a slave girl. He remembers Ruby from their days as children playing together and can barely believe how beautiful she has become. He is so attracted to the tall, willowy, slant-eyed woman that Ruby has grown into, he cannot take his eyes off her and decides she is perfect to exercise his masculine and master prerogatives.

Ruby notices him watching her, not so much all of her as her breasts, and she can feel his eyes upon her behind when she leaves the room. She tries to ignore his attention but he becomes bolder, asking her to serve him personally and touching her arm or hand, brushing the side of her breast.

One night after dinner is served Ruby takes the dirty linen out to the laundry house. As she opens the door, she is frightened almost out of her wits. She gasps, leaps back, dropping the linen. Bo stands in the corner smoking a cigarette. Once again she weaves her whole story for me.

"My, Ruby, haven't you grown up." Bo licks his lips and grabs his crotch.

"Massa Bo, I gots to git back to the house now," she begs.

Bo clutches her shoulders, pulls her so close that she smells the claret on his breath. He fondles her breasts.

"Please stop, Massa, I, uh, I gots my flowers on. Bleeding a whole lot. I'm a mess, could hardly get through dinner without spoiling myself."

"You ain't lying to me, are you?" asks Bo.

"No, sir" *I had to play this carefully,* she tells me. "Sir, I 'member you from when we's chillen. You still handsome." I'm already forming a plan, she adds to me.

"Well, you look like you ready. Got hips to have you a right fine little nigga. My daddy says it's time for me to spend some time in the quarters and I intend to start with my playmate Ruby."

"Yes, sir, Massa Bo. Bleeding be gone in a few days."

"Then, Ruby, let us meet here again after dinner for my dessert when you are ready," he winks as he leaves.

"As soon as Bo was out of earshot, Pearl, the old feelings of nausea overcame me. I retched and vomited like the days when the thought of playing with him made me sick. I am not going to have him touch me. I hate him."

"Oh, my Ruby." I sit up and pat my bed. She throws herself on me and I pat her back as she sobs. "I knew this was not a good idea. You insisted on working in the Big House. This is one of the reasons that I was uneasy about it. Out in the fields, you are not totally protected but you have a better chance of not being noticed. Now here you are, all dressed pretty, hair done up, and those white men crave slave women. Ruby, this is part of the reality of being enslaved. Remember, Master Bo believes he owns you. You are his to do with as he likes," I say.

"Yes, he says Master Ben told him it was time to have a slave girl."

"That bastard. He has done all of the raping he wants, now he is training his son to do the same thing." I sigh. It seems my life is one long sigh.

"Pearl, how come Master Ben and none of these white men haven't ever tried to have you?"

I look into the air, as if for an answer. "Whatever the reason, I am grateful," I say lightly and quickly bring the focus back to Ruby." When did you tell him your flowers would be gone?"

"I told him in a few days. I know he will be watching and waiting for me. Told him I would let him know," says Ruby.

"Let me sleep on this, Ruby."

Unable to, however, I stew all night, coming up with nothing. Early next morning I am sitting under the big oak tree sewing bandages when Ruby comes limping out. I rush to her.

"What's wrong with you, child? Did he bother you last night?"

"No, but I have a plan. I will tell you about it later."

That night, Ruby comes to my cabin. I am anxiously waiting up for her. "Now let me take a look at you. What is wrong?" I ask. Ruby then relates what occurred the night before.

"Last night I couldn't sleep and started thinking. I came up with a plan. I got up quietly so no one would hear me, pulled up my slip, picked up that hot poker and put it as close to my private parts as I could. I ain't never felt that kind of pain before. Wanted to scream but couldn't waken any of the other servants. I just held it there and let the tears stream down. When I looked, there was a big old welt."

"Let me see it! Oh my God, Ruby! What have you done?"

"I just gave myself the nigga disease," answers Ruby coolly.

"The nigga disease?"

"You will know soon enough." Ruby smiles and as soon as I get some salve on her, she leaves me as confused as ever.

Some three days later, Ruby combs her hair into a most attractive bun. Even puts a little honeysuckle on her bosom. She reveals to me her plan. I am afraid for her, but don't allow myself to intervene.

Ruby walks smugly into the sick house, a sly grin on her face. "Won't be working in the Big House anymore," she tells me as she sits on my bed. "And I definitely won't be the fancy of Bo." She throws her head back and lets out a jubilant laugh.

"How did it work?"

Ruby excitedly provides every detail of the encounter.

"True to my intention, I catch the eye of Bo and give him an *I'm ready* smile. He immediately calls me over to serve him more green beans. I bend down low enough for him to peek at my breasts and to smell the honeysuckle. Bo then deliberately spills his wine on the table cloth.

"'Ruby,' he orders.' When we are done eating, take this to the laundry house.'

"'Yessir, Massa Bo, right after ya'll finish yor dinner.'

"I clear the table and hurry to the laundry house. I pull up my dress, close my eyes, exhale deeply, and pierce the big welt with a small stick. Thick yellow pus runs down my leg. I hear Bo coming and quickly pull my dress down. He is breathing hard, hands ready to fondle me.

"'Come here, wench, lift up that skirt for Master Bo,' he demands. I purse my lips, with one hand open my bodice and touch my breast, while my other hand eases up my skirt. Bo starts to get all excited, unbuckles his pants, pulls them down a bit and suddenly stops.

"'What the hell?' He backs off. 'What is wrong with you, nigga? Where is all that pus coming from?'

"'Massa, I gots de nigga disease, dat's all. It don't hurt white folk, just niggas.'

"'Get away from me, you whore.' He knocks me to the floor. 'You think I want to have you, much less touch your diseased ass? Don't you ever come near me again. Don't even look at me. And this is your last night serving food. We don't want your nigga hands touching our food ever again.

Don't you ever come to the Big House. Back to the fields with you.'

"He hastily pulls up his pants and huffs from the laundry room.

"And I let out a big sigh of relief and smile to myself. No more Bo. Then I gather myself and hurry to tell you."

Ruby pulls up her skirt and shows me the oozing sore.

"Old Bo saw this and went crazy." She laughs." He wanted no part of me."

"Girl, you are something else," I say, having to laugh. "This looks pretty bad. Let me get it cleaned up." I go to my shelf and pull down a jar, get water and a cloth.

"You think he will be back?" I ask.

"Not in a hundred years. From the look on his face, he is more afraid of the nigga disease than death," Ruby says smiling as I clean the wound.

The next morning, Master Ben huffs into my cabin and inquires about the nigga disease in the quarters. Ruby listens from behind the screen and hears me assure him that I know who is infected, and it is not spreading through the quarters, but it will take some time for those infected to be cured. "Just have to be real careful with it, Massa."

"Pearl, I would prefer that Ruby not work in the sick house, especially not care for the men in here, while she is infected. Better she go to the fields."

'Yes, sir, Master Ben, whatever you think is best."

Ruby lets out a sigh of relief and says she looks forward to working in the fields again. Sadly the setting for her next drama.

Sam

Ruby's first day in the fields portends trouble with Sam the driver. As soon as the work day ends, Ruby rushes into the sick house, tears flowing down her cheeks. "Pearl, you have to help save me from this hell. My life is now the scorching sun, endless backbreaking bending, bloody hands, and worse of all, that devil Sam."

She describes the horrible day. "Pearl, Sam stands at the entrance to the cotton field scrutinizing each worker as he or she begins work. As I come up, he grabs my hand and pulls me aside. I actually jump and I know my eyes betray my fear of the one slave on the plantation I have been warned to avoid if at all possible.

"'Come here, gal, gotta make sure you learn how to pick some cotton.' I ease my hand out of his and keep my head lowered. 'What's your problem, girl? Got used to the Big House and think you too good for the fields?'

"Pearl, my heart is pounding, I swallow hard and say nothing, but I think, *What have I gotten myself into?*

"Two other girls new to the fields appear and Sam takes the same license of grabbing their hands and pulling them aside. He tells us to follow him, and he marches the three of us over to a tall, bent, dark, middle-aged woman wearing a head rag made of blue, red, and yellow patches. Her full mouth of white teeth glows when she smiles. She stretches out her arms to pull us near to her. Sam tells us, 'Sadie will show you how to pick cotton; she is one of the fastest.' He gives each of us a large sack and winks at me as he leaves. I shudder."

Sam is strikingly handsome, tall with green eyes, light brown skin and reddish brown hair. His good looks, however, are overshadowed by his arrogance, viciousness, and the mean whip he wears on his hip. He is not only the most powerful slave on the plantation but also the most hated slave in the quarters. Sam has the power to give higher quotas of cotton to pick each day or to assign additional tasks to those whom he dislikes or who anger him. He is even able to finagle the sale of those slaves with whom he has conflicts. Sam is hated by the male slaves and feared by the women. Sam has sired at least eight children in the quarters, all through sexual abuse of the women. Given his authority, Sam behaves and treats the enslaved women in the same manner as does Percy the overseer.

Because he is the son of an enslaved woman, Effie, and Richard Bellamy, one of two Bellamy sons of the founder of the plantation, he is both blessed and cursed. By his white blood, he is the light-skinned progeny who is heir to the Bellamy custom of being treated better than those slaves who are all black, thus creating a carefully designed division between field and house slaves.

His position of authority apparent in his light-skinned heritage has gone to his head and he finds that he does not fit anywhere, neither in the Big House nor in the quarters. He is encouraged to have any woman at any time he desires because he has white blood and will probably sire light children, children worth more because of that lightness. He lives at the edge of the quarters in a larger cabin than the others, wears better clothing, eats better food, and has liberal access to tobacco and liquor. Sam's privilege, however, cannot bring him peace of mind. Despite his lighter skin, he is a slave and has to answer to Percy the overseer and to Master Bellamy, his cousin. He spends his evenings and weekends alone and inebriated.

Ruby, disgusted by the way he treats the field hands, tells me more.

"Sam moves through the rows of cotton popping his whip and forcing the workers to move faster." 'Get a move on, niggas,' he yells. 'Don't let me have to help you work faster.'

"He stops at the spot where I am desperately trying to learn the rhythm of picking. I am totally frustrated; my fingers are not nimble, and I cannot catch or keep the pace of picking. As the others keep rhythm in swaying movement, I am awkward. Pearl, my fingers don't cooperate and rather than picking the cotton bud, just look." She shows me her pricked and bloody fingers.

"Pearl, Sam stands next to me and deliberately brushes up against me. You should see the smirk he gives me. With a devious smile he says, 'Gal, I'm going to have to work with you. Give you some personal attention.'"

Ruby shudders. "This sends chills through my body. My stomach sinks, and I know I am trapped in this situation due to own making."

I place my arms tightly around Ruby and hold her close. I guide her to my bed and we lay together, embracing each other as our tears drench the pillow. Ruby cries because she fears for her future, I weep because I am helpless. *There is nothing I can do to aid this poor child entrusted to my care.*

Cato

Ruby is aware that she cannot change the situation in which she now finds herself, but she quietly endures because she knows there is no change in sight. She does not complain about the aching back, sore fingers, or detestable Sam. I worry, though, that the self she has protected for so long is in danger. But to my delight and surprise, there comes a snatch of freedom in her life.

Feet pounding, eyes sparkling, Ruby bursts into the sick house to tell me about Cato. I can feel my face light up, delighted to see Ruby in such good cheer. She enters almost as if walking on air, face covered with a smile and bubbling with excitement. "Sit down Pearl." She ushers me to a chair. "The most exciting thing has happened." She proceeds to share every detail of the surprise of a man in her life. "Pearl, Cato came up to me and said, 'You are the sorriest cotton picker I've ever seen.' He teases me with a smile as he lifts a pile of cotton from his basket and places it into mine."

"'I take a shy glance at Cato and say, "'What?'"

"'You heard me,'" laughs Cato.

"'Well, thank you for the extra, but don't you need it for your own quota?'"

"'I've done my share for today. Do too much and they'll expect more. I pick just enough not to get the lash.'"

"I flash a wide smile to the tall, chestnut brown man. I admire his big brown eyes, high cheekbones and finely sculpted face."

"I say, 'I'm Ruby.'"

"'I'm Cato, helper to a cotton picker in need.' We both laugh.

"'Don't ever remember seeing you before,' I say.'

"'Haven't been here long, got sold, and Bellamy bought me,' says Cato.

"He looks at me, then smartly replies, 'But I've seen you. Heard about you, too. Got yourself kicked out of the Big House cause of some nigga disease. How in the hell did you come up with that?'

"Pearl, I could feel myself blushing. I shake my head and admit, 'Nigga disease is what niggas get when they're tired of waiting hand and foot on white folks.'

"Cato yelps."

Ruby continues."'Seriously, that slimy Bo tried to hem me up in the laundry house, was all I could think of at the time.'

"'You are one clever girl.'

"He has a big smile on his face when he asks me if I live with the midwife Pearl.

"'Why do you know so much about me?' I ask, smiling of course.

"'You are famous. I've been keeping my eye on you since I came here,' teases Cato. 'Pearl let you out with boys?'

"'Hush, I'm a woman now, do what I please.'" She shows me how she purses her lips and places her hands on her hips. I throw my head back in laughter; this is my Ruby.

"Cato can't help but laugh and then says to me, 'Listen to you, grown woman. Okay, so how about Saturday after we leave the fields we walk down to the creek?'

"'I love being in the woods; it's the only place I feel free,' I tell him.

"We agreed that after we come in from the field on Saturday, we are going for a picnic in the woods." Ruby is so excited, she even offers to gather food for a picnic. Of course I help her to make this a very special afternoon.

"Well, he must be a special young man. I've never seen you like this before. And I always felt you thought those woods belonged just to you," I say. Ruby looks down and smiles.

"Might even make a good husband; you know Master is keen on all the young women finding a man," I tease.

"Yeah, sure,"answers Ruby as she rolls her eyes and grins.

~~~~~~~~~~~~~~

On Saturday, Ruby puts on her favorite blue calico dress and the pretty bonnet with the red band. Cato knocks quietly on the door. l look him up and down and nod to him to come in.

"Hello, Cousin Pearl." He gives me a small bow.

"What a gentleman you are," I say, as he smiles handsomely. "So you are new on the plantation, aren't you?"

Cato smiles and admits he has been sold away from the Andrews plantation.

"Overseer said I had a bad attitude, didn't smile enough. When I told him there wasn't anything to smile about, I found myself here."

"And Bellamy bought you?" I ask a little incredulous.

"Well, I smiled plenty at the sale, showed all my teeth and muscles. Besides, the prettiest girls are on Bellamy." He winks at Ruby.

"Ruby has made a nice picnic lunch. Have a good time."

I watch Ruby lead the way as she and Cato walk slowly into the woods.

~~~~~~~~~~~~~~

When she returns in the evening her face is aglow. I feel that something has changed within her. She is a different Ruby. For the first time, she talks to me like a big sister, however much I have thought of her as that over the years. I remember clear as day her joy as she shared every detail.

"Pearl, we come to a clearing full of tall grass and wild flowers, we can hear the sounds of birdcalls drifting through the air and the clean, fresh smell of it all fills our nostrils. It was wonderful."

"'This is my favorite place," I say. 'I come here when I want to get in touch with the inside of me.'

"Cato looks deeply into my eyes and says, 'You are not like the other girls in the quarters.'

"'Just being myself,' I say.

"'You got a man?' asks Cato.

"'No, you got a girl?'

"'How would you like to be my girl?'

"I look into those sparkling brown eyes of his and study his smooth dark skin and say, 'I'll think about it.'"

"'Just don't think too long. You are special, Ruby,' he says as he pulls me into him and hugs me gently.

"Pearl, the closeness of our bodies made me experience things I never felt before. I take a deep breath, anticipating what will come next, and Cato plants a tiny kiss on my lips. We sit side by side, arms around our knees and talk about things we have never broached to another living thing."

"As the sun begins to set, we leave the woods, and as we walk, I say, "'I will be your girl.'"

"'Took you long enough to say so.'"

"'I was just giving your proposal full consideration.' We both just look at each other and break out in laughter."

~~~~~~~~~~~

After that first afternoon, Ruby and Cato spend every free minute they can together. Cato's presence in Ruby's life softens her emotions and mannerisms. There is again a lightness and determination in her spirit. She tells me she likens his skin to being luscious as a fresh blackberry, and I figure they are a couple now. Each day in the fields, Cato waits for Ruby and slyly eases handfuls of cotton into her basket. They giggle at their secret. Ruby admires Cato's spirit of defiance. He reminds her of Roy who must be living free now. While picking, Ruby shields her eyes from the sun and searches for Cato among the other male hands and waves across the rows to him.

They spend every Saturday afternoon together in the woods, talking, fishing, picking berries, sharing corn cakes. On Sundays, Ruby and Cato sit far away from the others. She tells me that when the minister exalts the slaves to mind their masters, they nudge each other and mimic the subservience required of slaves. "Yassah, Massa, I be's a good slave."

Some nights they slip out and sit under the big oak tree to watch the stars. Ruby has never been happier. She wonders what life could be with him off the plantation. Snatching little bits of freedom with Cato makes living enslaved a little easier.

Those moments spent with Cato do not go unnoticed, however. Sam, who has intentions of his own for Ruby, keeps a watchful eye.

~~~~~~~~~~~~~

About two months after their first walk in the woods, Ruby's sleep cannot contain her restless mind. She wakes me. I still feel more like a big sister and friend rather than mother these days. She tells me the seriousness of their conversation they had tonight. As usual, she relates her time with Cato like a story.

"'Let's sit here, Ruby,'" Cato says as he spreads a cloth on the ground. I cast my eyes down and feel my chest tighten. What can be wrong?

"'Ruby, I really like very much. But I must be honest with you. I can't be a husband to you. I plan to run as soon as I can.'

"Pearl, my heart drops and I feel suddenly frightened.

"'Won't marry any woman until I'm free. Seen too many men love a woman, then he or she is sold, and he just grieves and drinks himself almost to death. I really care for you, Ruby, but it's hard loving the way that we are.'

"I come close to Cato's ear, stroke his hair and whisper, 'I understand. I only ask that you take me with you. I don't belong here. I will never get used to being a slave, just isn't in me.'"

As Ruby is telling me this, I am shaking inside. I fear what I will hear next.

"'Would you really run with me, Ruby? Would you leave Pearl?'

"'Yes, Cato, I will do anything to be with you.'

"'Really, Ruby?' We look deeply into each other's eyes.

"'That would make me the happiest man in the world,' Cato says and gently kisses my lips.

"'Yes, Cato. I will miss Pearl, but yes, I will go with you.'"

I listen and a chill falls over me. Deep within, I know that my precious Ruby will actually leave me, even knowing that this is so often the way of things. Then, Ruby shares the most intimate of details about the evening.

"'Cato takes me into his arms and we lie on the soft grass. He cautiously places his hand on my covered breasts, unbuttons my bodice and slides his

113

hand inside and strokes my raised nipples. Shivers of passion course through my body as my head fells back on the cloth, and a satisfied moan escapes my lips. Cato lifts my skirt and gently glides his hand up my leg. He touches then kisses the scar on my thigh. Cato raises his head and pretends to be frightened. 'I won't catch the nigga disease, will I?'

"We both laugh, and I playfully smack his cheek, then kiss him there. 'Wouldn't be here now if it wasn't for the nigga disease.' Breathing heavily, Cato slowly massages my private parts.

"My head falls back on the broad tree trunk as a streak of white light flashes behind my closed eyes, and I feel as if my whole being is released. I climb on top of Cato and plant tiny kisses over his face and neck and suddenly loosen his pants. Cato takes my hand and guides me, as I lovingly help him release his pent–up passion. We touch, kiss, caress, and release hot, sweet love juices until we both are satisfied. Together we lie in each other's embrace, resting from our spent passion.

"Our bodies want more. We strip off clothing and we are flesh to flesh. As Cato enters me, I bolt up and say fiercely, 'I can't have a slave baby!'

"Cato grabs my shoulders and nods in agreement. 'I will not let that happen, Ruby. We

114

can't run if we have a child. We will give each other pleasure, but no baby until we are free. I promise you.'

"I smile as he reassures me. I lie down and guide Cato back into my body. In a few seconds, Cato moans deeply, and quickly pulls himself from me. His seed spills upon the grass. I cradle his head as tears flow down my face."

Discomfort wells in me as I listen. *This is my little girl, the baby that I helped to birth, who has now become a woman.* There is also a slight pang of envy. *I have never experienced the feelings Ruby is describing, and I have no hopes that I ever will.*

Ruby tells me she told Cato about Roy and how she has yearned for freedom since that time. And she tells Cato, "From the first day in the woods, I knew that I would never want to be with any man other than you. Your rebellion against this unholy state in which we are kept, and just hearing that you want to be free, makes me feel like you have spoken to my heart."

Cato's rebellious spirit speaks to Ruby's longing and her hopes. She sees much of herself in him, the child without a father or mother to raise him, never feeling that he was meant to be a slave, living in the quarters but not finding his place there.

She loves to hear stories he tells about the men when they gather. They joke and pride themselves on their small acts of rebellion -- leaving the gate open so the cows can wander off, breaking farm tools, or just pretending they are too sick to work. They talk of "freeing" the Massa's cows, pigs, and chickens, but not themselves. Like Cato, they want to be free, but the yolk of enslavement bears down too heavily upon them. Most of all, they love their wives and children and cannot bear to be separated from them. They cannot stand to inflict the same suffering upon themselves or their loved ones as the slave master. Love and loving is a perilous act for the enslaved, especially for the man. He is property like a cow, horse, or bag of rice. He cannot protect the object of his love, nor can he prevent her sale or the sale of the products of their love.

Life is as good as it can be for a slave girl as Ruby discovers happiness. But the love of the enslaved is always overshadowed by the fact of their bondage, their ownership by another, the possibility of the sale of the beloved. Ruby knows that falling in love with Cato can be dangerous, possibly opening her heart to future sadness, but in this moment, her body and mind cannot care

Ruby tells me that she holds an image of her beloved in her head, imagines herself right beside him, and whispers *I love you*, into his ear. She sighs, closes her eyes and contents herself with the pact the lovers have made to give each other sweet release, a little grab of freedom, while they make plans to escape. She loves Cato deeply, a love freely chosen, given, and reciprocated. Love lifts and frees her spirit. For the enslaved, love and family affirm our humanity. When we love, we defy the lies told about us; that we are no more than animals, that we do not experience human emotions.

Cato Is Gone

Passion drives Ruby and Cato to take risks that will eventually lead to disaster. Their desire to see and to give pleasure to each other outweighs the fatigue of long days spent in the field and the danger of being discovered. Ruby and Cato sneak into the woods after Percy the overseer makes his rounds to ensure the quarters is asleep. One night, thinking that I am asleep, Ruby slips from her bed, waiting until she sees Cato head for the woods. She jumps when she hears me speak.

"I see you, Ruby. I know when you leave. I have a bad feeling about you meeting Cato tonight."

"We will be fine, we are careful."

"If Percy catches you, both of you will be lashed or worse."

Ruby leans down and kisses me on the cheek.

"I love you, Pearl. I will be careful. I won't get any of us into trouble." She slips out of the cabin.

~~~~~~~~~~~~~~~

I cannot sleep. A sense of dread covers me like a quilt.

Before long, Ruby returns. "Pearl, please wake up," she cries.

"What is it, my girl?"

"I think somebody has been watching us. I believe they heard us talking about running away."

"Tonight, I sensed something might happen. I warned you to be careful. Tell me.

As she usually does, Ruby provides every detail of her time with Cato, and as she speaks, I can clearly see the scene that she describes.

"Cato is standing naked in the moonlight, his taut dark body glistening. I stand for a moment, admiring, and then I tear off my night shift and run into his arms.

"'My sweet, sweet Ruby,' he whispers into my ears.

"'My darling Cato, I hate every minute that I am not with you,' I whisper sweetly into his.

"'How much longer, Cato? Each day in this place is a living hell. I hate the way Sam watches me.

"'Not long now. I have gathered most of what we need. We'll be ready soon. Figure in a month we will be out of here. Damn sure don't mean for us to freeze to death in the field this winter.'

"We caress and plant kisses over each other's bodies. I moan as my breasts are fondled and Cato groans as I give him pleasure. Cato is careful to release his seed on the ground. As we begin to passionately make love again, we are startled by the sound of a moving bush.

"'What is that?' I say. I am instantly frightened.

"'Probably just a deer." Cato continues to passionately kiss me. He is about to spill his seed when we hear the sound of voices among the bushes.

"'Oh, my God, Cato,' I whisper.

"Someone is there, they have been watching us. Cato abruptly stops all movement and holds me tightly. We listen intently but hear only the sounds of insects and animals rustling.

"'Hurry, get dressed.' Cato pulls on his pants and starts toward the bushes.

"'It's okay, I don't see anything,' he says.

"'Cato, I am scared. Suppose someone heard us talking about running away. Before I left, Pearl warned me to be careful.' I begin to cry.

"'Don't worry, my sweet Ruby. We are safe. Better get back, though. 'Don't want you to fall asleep and slice your foot with that hoe tomorrow.' He smiles, touches my lips with his finger, and Pearl, we hold each other in the longest, deepest embrace. Then he says to me, 'You go first, I will be right behind you.' Cato holds me by the shoulders and looks into my teary eyes. 'I think it is time for us to run,' he says. 'Gather what you can, and come Saturday we will kiss Bellamy Plantation goodbye.'

"'I love you, Cato.'

"Then I run through the woods and back to you."

Ruby and I talk most of the night. We have just fallen asleep, Ruby on my bed, when the bell rings for the field workers to line up for their tools. Ruby throws on her shift and heads out with the others.

~~~~~~~~~~~

That afternoon, Ruby slips into the sick house, her eyes puffy and red. She tells me how she has spent much of the day searching for Cato. She tells me that she doesn't see Cato among the men who are walking ahead and when she reaches the field he is nowhere in sight. She nervously scans the field as best she can in the morning mist. Her heart begins to pound as she is overtaken by fear. Something is wrong."Where is Cato?" she asks, her voice shaking.

"During the lunch break, I hurried over to where the men are eating," she explained. "'Have you seen Cato? Where is Cato?'"

"'You mus' 'bout kill de man las' night, ain't seen him dis mornin',' one of Cato's housemates volunteers.

"'Yeh, Ruby, he hidin' somewhere, too tired to come to de field today, maybe you best check the sick house,' another laughs.

"'No, ma'am, aint' seen him dis mornin',' frowns another. 'Ain't like him.'

All day, Ruby looks for and asks about Cato.

"Pearl, something is terribly wrong. Cato has not been seen all day. I am going to his cabin now to see what I can find out." I go with her to where the single men live. When we arrive, Sam is standing on the stoop.

"He ain't here and his stuff is gone too. Looks like he done run off."

I look at Ruby, Sam's shocking words strike her like a blow. She stares unbelieving and starts to collapse. Sam catches her.

"Hey, better get you over to Pearl's. You don't look too well." Ruby can hardly walk, she can't catch her breath. She tries to pull away from Sam. I reach for her but he pushes me aside. When we reach the sick house, Ruby jerks away from Sam, falls into my arms and weeps uncontrollably.

"Cato is gone, Pearl, my Cato is gone."

"Yeah, looks like he done run off," Sam drawls. "Just up and gone. You weren't planning to run with him were you?" He smiles at Ruby. "Think you better forget about him and find yourself another man."

I give Sam a dirty look as I cradle the weeping Ruby in my arms as I glare at him. "There is no need for that kind of talk. Can't you see the girl is in pain? You can leave now; I will take care of her." I point Sam to the door.

I guide Ruby to my bed and help the weak and pitiful girl out of her shift. "Lie down, Ruby. Just take some deep breaths." I gather a bowl of warm water, wipe her face, arms, legs, feet and then gently cover her. Ruby is sobbing hysterically and all I can do is hold her tightly in my arms and kiss her forehead. I feel powerless, the person I love most in the world I cannot protect or soothe. I call to Lizzie from Auntie Ama's to help me with the other patients. I spend the rest of the evening and all night simply holding Ruby to my heart. Finally I am able to get her to drink some calming tea.

Ruby stays rolled into a protective cocoon. She refuses all but the barest amount of food and tea that I force down her. I imagine that Ruby plays the last embrace with Cato over and over in her mind. She keeps repeating, "Something is wrong, something has happened to Cato. He would not leave me." Then Ruby descends into a dark space where there are no tears, only infinite sadness. She holds her stomach as if a burning emptiness has overtaken her. Only sleep rescues her from the breaking of her heart.

After a week, Percy stops in the sick house to check on Ruby's condition. "Time for that gal to get back to work, been a week now." I lie to him. I motion him to come near her bed.

"She has a terrible fever, see I put these leaves on her forehead every day to draw it out, but it's taking a while. She will be better soon."

I tell the other women who come to visit that Ruby is either asleep or too sick to be disturbed. One visitor, however, comes every day. Sam inquires about Ruby's health and insists that by now she should be able to return to the fields.

"If that gal isn't better by the beginning of next week, might have to talk to Master Ben about selling her. Can't afford to have her around if she can't work. You know what I mean?"

I can feel the fire in my eyes. "How dare you? This poor girl is suffering, have you no heart? What kind of man are you?"

"I have the same blood as you, Sista," Sam retorts snidely. I spit on the floor in disgust.

"I'll be back tomorrow," he says.

I prepare Ruby another cup of tea and sit beside her bed.

"Ruby, we must talk. Please listen to me. I am afraid of what will happen if you do not snap out of this."

Ruby uncovers her head and takes a sip of the steaming tea. Tears flood my eyes and flow down my cheeks. I grasp her shoulders and look into her sad, red, puffy eyes.

"Ruby, you know how much I love you. You are like my daughter. I don't think I can stand to lose you. So please hear me out." Ruby sits up, sniffles and nods that she will listen.

"Ruby, this is the reality of the life of the enslaved. You have resisted your state since you were born. Now you understand that for us nothing is permanent, love often disappears in the night, and in the daylight only despair remains. We are expected to carry the pain and go on."

"No," says Ruby weakly. "How can I go on, Pearl? I love Cato as much as I love freedom. Loving him was the only snatch of freedom I had. How can you ask me to just give up on love or freedom? It's not possible."

"This is the reality of our lives, Ruby. You will survive. Look at all of the women in the quarters that have lost their men. They wake at night, reach for him, and cry themselves back to sleep. Most hold on to some small token of their love, a button, and ribbons he has given her, or they put away a dress that he loved to see her wear as a reminder of his love for her. Some like poor Blanche have lost both man and child to the slave market. She goes on."

Tears gush from Ruby's eyes as she tries to catch her breath. I wrap her in my arms and we both weep until there are no tears left to cry.

"Ruby, love in the quarters is fleeting, only for the moment for most. I saw the joy in your eyes, the glow on your face, and I was so happy for you. But deep inside, I worried that you too would have to suffer the pain of so many enslaved women. Ruby, I am so sorry."

Ruby tightens her arms around me, lifts her head, and asks. "Pearl, have you ever loved a man?"

I start to cry again. "No, Ruby, at least you have known a man's love. And you had a love you freely chose. I expect that I will live my life as a midwife like my Granny Abena who raised me. I will never know love or have the love of a man. In many ways, I have learned about love through your loving Cato. It seems as though my purpose is to bring the fruit of other's love into the world."

"But don't you want love? These few months with Cato have been freedom for me. I want that for you. Pearl, I love you too. I love you so much. You *are* like a mother to me. I am sorry for all the times I have been difficult and made you worry."

"Ruby, I wish many times that I was as brave as you." I squeeze next to Ruby on the bed and we fall asleep in each other's embrace.

We are awakened by a tap on the door. "What is that?" asks Ruby as she bolts up in the bed. I slowly rise and go to the door. "Who is it?" I ask.

"It's Jacob, Cousin Pearl. I know it very late, but I have somethin' to tell Ruby. It's very important. Please let me in." I open the door and stand back, afraid of what the aged butler has come to say to Ruby.

128

"Please be quiet and don't wake the others."
I lead Jacob back to Ruby's bed. Ruby gives Jacob
an annoying look.

"What do you want?" she asks curtly.

"I hear my little oyster stew is not doing so
well." Ruby half smiles. "I have some news for you.
It's not exactly good news but I hope it will ease you
mind and make you feel better."

"Okay, what is it? Is it about Cato?" Jacob
nods and Ruby holds her breath.

"Somebody in the quarters alerted Percy,
told him you and Cato were slipping off every night.
Told Percy that Cato was spilling his seed on the
ground. So Percy starts watching and waiting for y'all
to go to the woods. Saw y'all the night Cato
disappeared. Master Ben said a young girl like you
should be having plenty of babies. Said you and Cato
were stealing from him, by not having a baby. Master
Ben was furious. Said y'all had to be sold. Decided to
sell Cato, said he would find you a husband and put
an end to this foolishness. Promised you will be with
child before winter." Ruby and I sit with our
mouths and eyes wide open.

"Grabbed Cato right after y'all left the
woods, brought him to the Big House, and woke
Master up. Percy took him into town to the holding

cell that very night, sold him the next day. Sold him down South, Mississippi. Master says he won't have slaves stealing his profits and what y'all did was thievery. Sorry, Ruby, but that's what I just heard."

Ruby, too weak to stand, motions Jacob to lean over. She gives him a hug. "Thank you, Jacob. At least I know what happened to my love." He hugs her back. "Jacob, I am sorry for all of the hard times I gave you when I was in the Big House."

"Ain't nothing, Ruby. I understand you better than you think."

"But, Jacob, just one more thing, I will not have a slave baby, no matter what Master Ben says."

"I hear you, Ruby." He smiles and closes the cabin door behind him.

I look at Ruby and shake my head. Looks like through it all, my Ruby has kept herself.

A Bit of Light

"Hurry, Ruby, time to go. Why, you are not even dressed?" I sigh.

"Pearl, I don't feel so good, think my flowers are about to come on. Let me gather my strength today, you know I have to be back in the fields tomorrow," a downcast and pitiful Ruby responds. I laugh to myself. *Ruby sees her flowers more than any girl I know. They appear any time it's convenient.*

"Alright, I left breakfast for you," I say as I head out the door to join Auntie Ama and the cluster of women outside the cabin ready to go to the preaching. "Where's Ruby?" inquires Auntie Ama.

"She needs time to gather herself before going to the field tomorrow."

Shaking her head, Auntie Ama says, "Dat gal always doing the opposite of what is expected."

~~~~~~~~~~~~

Auntie Ama and I sit wringing our hands and staring at each other, wondering where Ruby can be. It is almost dusk. Finally she glides into the room, humming, face aglow. Oblivious to the gloom in the room, she is bubbly as she tells Auntie Ama and me about her day. She sits at our feet and excitedly begins. I imagine the beauty of her day as she weaves her story.

"I wait until the quarter's street is free of chatter and feet shuffling along before I leave the cabin." She mimics her feelings and movements as she tells her story. "I peek out of the cabin door in both directions before stepping outside." Ruby's eyes are sparkling as she proudly tells of her cleverness. "I skip down the quarter's street onto the path into the woods. When I reach the edge, I stop for a moment, hug myself, take a big breath and absorb the freedom this haven always provides me. It is such a beautiful freedom, I feel a sense of lightness as I breathe in the damp woodsy air. I smell the lavender and honeysuckle. A baby deer creeps close to watch me, and I turn to see a fat brown rabbit whose wide-eyed stare appears to say, 'Welcome home.' A flock of birds descends and their chirping calls my name, 'Ruby, Ruby.' I turn my face to the sun and with outstretched hands I dance in circles until I fall dizzy onto the soft grass. It is in this place, surrounded by the fragrance of lavender and honeysuckle, the sounds of crickets and the gentle movement of animals that my spirit comes alive again. I find the strength to endure the loss of my beloved Cato."

Auntie Ama and I sit, our eyes fixed on Ruby as she transports us into the change in her.

"I step lightly to seek out the place where Cato and I shared love." Now tears fill Ruby's eyes. "I kneel and press my lips to the spot. The moist grass embraces my face. I tip my head back and close my eyes. As tears stream down, my heart feels full and I am overcome by gratitude. In this very spot, I shared love with Cato. In loving Cato I found a sense of freedom. I raise my palms to the sky. 'Thank you for sending Cato into my life.'"

Tears roll down my and Auntie Ama's cheeks, we are overtaken by the beauty and the deepness of the feelings Ruby is expressing.

It is as if she is still there in the woods, still in her moments of pure freedom. She has always been able to go to a place of freedom within, a place where none of the enslaved, including myself seem capable of doing. *Well, she and Auntie Mina,* I think to myself.

Ruby continues her story. "After a while, I walk deeper into the woods. The tall oak trees wear silver moss like shawls as slivers of sunlight peek through their branches. I remove my shoes and dip my feet into the cool creek. Almost as in a dream, I smile to myself as I imagine Cato turning to show me the fish he has caught for our dinner." She acts out the next scene. "I call him over to me, press a kiss on his cheeks, pop blackberries into his waiting mouth and lick the sweet juice that escapes from his lips."

There is more. "I spread a cloth and recline between the long roots of an oak, I lean my head against the broad trunk, and a warmth sweeps over my entire being. I remember the passionate moments I spent here with Cato. 'Thank you, Cato, for sharing this bit of freedom with me.'" Ruby shows us how she blows a kiss into the air and I can see her chest swell with joy and pride. I know in my heart that Ruby will not be one of those sad women in the quarters. She freely chose her lover, felt his embrace, and their passion flowed like a furious river. She made a vow to herself and to Cato never to bring a child into this brutal and inhuman world of enslavement, and she shall keep that vow. In the bower of nature, Ruby feels a freedom that no one can take from her. Nothing from the quarters or the Big House can touch her there. She is free.

"I actually drift off to sleep remembering my sweet Cato. When I awaken, the sun is setting. Even the sunset is beautiful. Everything about this day has filled my heart with joy. I gather my things and head back to the quarters. So here I am."

As Ruby finishes telling her story, she realizes that she has stepped into a room heavy with sadness. Now, she notices Auntie Ama sitting with her head bowed and my face etched with distress.

"What's wrong, Pearl?" asks a suddenly anxious Ruby. I look at Auntie Ama, shake my head, hesitantly speak.

"Master Ben made an announcement after service today." I cannot look Ruby in the eyes.

"What is it, Pearl? Announcement about what?"

I take a deep breath.

"What, Pearl, what?" insists Ruby.

"Master Ben said that Sam will jump the broom next Saturday. Master is planning a big celebration, roasting a pig, all kinds of food, fiddle playing, dancing...."

"So, why are you so upset?" asks a confused Ruby.

I bite my lip. "Master said that Sam will jump the broom with you next Saturday."

Ruby gasps, unable to catch her breath, wide-eyed. She blurts out, "With me?" She folds limply into a kneeling position, unbelieving. "Jump the broom with Sam? You can't mean that."

Auntie Ama rises from the chair, comes over and places one arm around Ruby and fans her with the other hand.

"Chile, may not be so bad. Sam favors you and Massa favors Sam. Might make yor life easier in the end," says Auntie Ama.

"Yes, Ruby...." I start. But Ruby's shock turns to anger.

"I'm not going to marry him. I'll run away first."

"Ruby, you are going to have to marry Sam. Master says it's time for Sam to marry and for you to start to have babies. He's not going to change his mind. You must accept this."

"No, I don't," she yells and runs out the door. I watch and listen as she rushes into Sam's cabin without knocking and throws the door open wide. We see him sitting at the table with a glass of whiskey in hand. He looks up and smiles broadly. Worried, Auntie Ama and I stand on my stoop trying hard to hear the conversation.

"Why, Ruby, so nice to see you. Sit down. Missed you in service today. Have you heard the good news?"

I image Ruby staring at Sam with eyes as cold as winter.

"Girl, we are gonna jump the broom next Saturday. Master Ben has given his blessings. Going to kill a pig and have a big feast. Master Ben says the women in the kitchen house are going to make all kinds of good foods."

Still we hear no words fall from Ruby's lips.

"Oh, I take it you are not happy, huh? But you will be, better than being sold South, don't know what kind of situation you could find yourself in. Better to be Sam's wife."

Still no response from Ruby.

"You're gon to be the wife of the driver, the most powerful nigga on this plantation. You'll live better than anybody else in the quarters. We gonna have a bunch of little ones to make master proud. You are a good woman, Ruby, a little stubborn, but you can make a man proud."

We are aghast as we see Ruby step toward Sam, look him directly in the eyes, spit on the floor and turn to leave. Sam grabs her roughly and turns her around to face him. Auntie Ama and I hold each other in fear of what will happen next.

"You will soon forget about that common field nigga. He couldn't give you what I can."

Ruby pulls away, places her hands on her hips, stands in the doorway and finally speaks.

"I won't forget Cato, and you and Master may force me to jump the broom, but mind you, Sam, I will never be a wife to you, and I will die before I have a slave baby."

Auntie Ama and I quickly go into the sick house as Ruby turns to leave. She runs inside the sick house. Ignoring the wide-eyed patients, she screams, "Pearl, what am I going to do?" I grab hold of her and hug her. She slumps in my arms. "I can't jump the broom with Sam, Auntie. I can't even stand the sight of him. I know he was behind Cato being sold. Will you please talk to Master Ben and convince him to change his mind?" Auntie Ama and I shepherd Ruby into a private corner away from the patients.

"Ruby, you know what Jacob told you. It is Sam or something worse. I can't bear to see you sold." I start to cry.

"Ruby, most women in the quarters did not choose their husband," Auntie Ama says. "Master put them with the man he felt could produce lots of children. Some do come to love the man. You might even come to love Sam."

"I will never love Sam, and he will get a poor wife, I'll make sure of that. For all I care, Master can make his own babies; none will come from this body."

"Chile, quit that kind of talk," warns Auntie Ama.

"You won't be so angry next Saturday," I say as I hold her face in my hands.

Ruby looks deeply into my eyes. "Pearl, I may be a poor slave girl, owning nothing in this world that you can see. I don't own my labor or where I sleep. All that I own is way deep inside of me, my love and my womb. The only freedom a slave girl like me has is who I will give my love to and what seeds I will allow to grow in my womb. I will only love one man in this life and this womb will only bring a free child into this world."

The Wedding

The sprawling lawn behind the Big House is covered with tables that mimic summer with sprays of yellow swamp sunflowers, purple cornflowers, and the deep green holly fern. The aroma of pig roasting on a spit fills the air. House slaves busily lay out bowls of steaming okra stew, red rice, and potato salad. Platters are filled with roasted wild duck and corn pone. A table set aside especially for desserts holds scrumptious-looking pound cake, custards, and sweet potato pone.

Master Ben has taken pains to ensure that today is a special day for the quarters. He has sanctioned the marriage of Sam the driver and Ruby, a couple that he feels has great potential to produce many healthy offspring. This wedding in particular celebrates Master Ben's encouragement of marriage and children. Today, the quarters is allowed to leave work an hour earlier so that they can prepare for the festivities. The women wear their finest outfits -- weddings are special occasions. It is a brief, sanctioned relief from work, a time to eat, laugh, sing, and dance into the morning hours. And there is no church service the next day.

The fiddlers take their positions and began to play a jig. A soft and steady mumble flows through the crowd and occasionally a hearty laugh.

"Ruby jumping the broom with Sam, I'll believe it when I sees it, "laughs Sally.

"Won't happen 'les Massa make her and den dat gon be hard to do," agrees Susie.

"Dat fool is crazy, dat girl don' want him," snorts Hannah.

"Ain't no man dat gal gone love 'cept Cato and dey done gone and sold him," adds Puddin, one of Cato's cabin mates.

The crowd becomes quiet when Master Ben and Mistress Charlotte appear on the porch of the Big House. A hush falls as Sam approaches the spot where he and Ruby are to stand. Sam is handsome in his dark coat and gray pants with a yellow swamp sunflower tucked in his lapel. He takes a deep breath and looks toward the quarter's road where he is expecting to see Ruby emerge any minute. Everyone waits in anticipation for the bride-to-be.

Minutes pass and no Ruby. Sam casts an impatient eye around the group. Auntie Ama and I exchange glances. She had not let me help her dress. What is she up to? Women tuck their heads together in clusters and men turn to whisper in each other's ears. Sam looks up at Master Ben who is looking serious and then back at the slaves whose subdued but constant chatter is like the humming of bees when they find a honey cone, a constant, and rising in intensity.

Finally Ruby emerges. The quarters all look and strain to see what she is wearing. Hands go up to cheeks, contorted frowns cover faces, and some heads just shake in disbelief. A loud gasp comes from the crowd the closer she gets, and the women cover their mouths as they giggle and mumble to each other. The men, out of respect, turn their faces toward the ground. No one will look at Sam as he turns to see Ruby with four uncombed plaits flying in all directions. She wears a ragged work shift and saunters barefoot, carries a twig in her arms like a bouquet. She steps up beside Sam and in front of Master Ben and Miss Charlotte. Ruby is ready to jump the broom.

"What the hell is this?" rages Sam. "Are you crazy? Why do you look like this on your wedding day? Why aren't you fixed up? Look at your hair!" Sam raises his hand to slap Ruby but stops short when he remembers Master Ben is watching.

Massa Ben quickly inquires, "Ruby, why you are in your work shift? You can have more time to dress properly. We will wait for you. This is your special day."

Ruby's answer stuns even him. "I's a slave and I's doin what I's told. Ain't dis part of my work?"

Master Ben steps back and shakes his head. He sighs. "Well, let's get on with the ceremony. " His face takes on a serious expression and he intones, like the minister on Sundays, "Sam, do you take this woman to be your wife?"

Sam, breathing heavily, sweat covering his face, says a quick, "Yassir, I do."

"Ruby, do you take this man to be your husband?"

"Yassir, Massa, dis my husband."

"Then you may jump the broom!"

Sam grabs for Ruby's hand, which she pulls away as quickly as their feet touch the ground on the other side of the broom. They face each other, cold eye to cold eye, knowing this will be a most unhappy union.

A weak scatter of applause comes from the crowd, and they all move quickly to the tables filled with food. They ooh and ah as they take huge helpings of everything. Master Ben and Miss Charlotte disappear into the Big House as the fiddlers

144

begin to play. Sam drags Ruby behind him, headed to his cabin. Worried, Auntie Ama and I head back to the sick house. We sit on my stoop and listen to the newly married couple's yelling argument.

As they move toward the open window, Sam pulls Ruby up to him by her shoulders. "How dare you shame me like this? I have a good mind to give you a good beating right now."

"Go ahead, but remember how Master doesn't like his slave women beat unless they are getting the lash."

"You think you are special, don't you? But you are a slave gal just like every other one of you on this plantation. You are owned by Master Ben and if he says you marry me, you have no choice."

I watch Ruby hold her head back and turn it to the side to guard her sense of personal space.

"I am here, ain't I? What more do you want?"

"I want you to stop your insolence, to apologize to me, and to act like a wife. I am not playing with you, Ruby. You take on your wifely duties or you will find yourself South before you know it."

"So, is that where you sent Cato?"

"Cato is a common field nigga. You were too good for him. I can give you what he never could. I already have a new job for you at the dairy. You, my wife, no longer have to labor in the fields. Look at this cabin, it is better than most. Got somebody to grow your garden. You can dress better than any woman in the quarters. Ruby I am the most important man in the quarters and I chose you for my wife. I have favored you since I first saw you come to the fields. I just want you to be a wife to me. In time you will come to love me. I am a patient man."

"You sent away the only man I will ever love, and he is far from being a common 'field nigga,'" retorts Ruby. "You sent my Cato away and I will always hate you for that."

Ruby's anger seems to have the opposite effect of what she hopes. Sam appears to find her spirited insults sensual. "Get your clothes off. You are my wife now. Show me some of that passion where it matters," says Sam.

Auntie Ama and I are shocked by what Ruby does next. We hear her stomping her feet and acting as though she is going into a fit of some sort. From her open cabin window, we watch as she flays her arms, jerks her head back and forth, and screams to the top of her lungs. At first Sam stands back in shock, but spying us on my stoop and fearing that the whole quarters can hear her, he grabs Ruby's arms and wrestles her to the floor.

Each night for the first weeks of the marriage, as Sam approaches Ruby, she throws a fit. With seemingly little hope of consummating his marriage, Sam appeals to me. "You must let Ruby know that she will be a wife to me or she will be sold." It takes more than the urging of Sam and me to make the stubborn Ruby perform her wifely duties.

"I Have Not Seen My Flowers"

"Pearl, I have not seen my flowers. Help me please," pleads a weeping Ruby. "This awful thing cannot be happening to me. I will not bear a slave child," Ruby says.

"Hush, dear, how long has it been?" I question.

"Master Ben came to the cabin a month ago and forced us to perform the act in his presence, says I should be with child by now. My stomach churned with each thrust. Sam satisfied himself, and I vomited afterward.

"Old Ben said, 'I'm looking for some babies from you, Ruby. Hadn't been for Sam marrying you, you'd be picking cotton somewhere in Mississippi by now, maybe even Texas. Have some babies now. Sam, don't make me put you in the fields, you are the man of this house, produce me some babies, one a year.'" Ruby added that she vomited again after Ben left.

"Pearl, you must know what to do, help me please," Ruby begs.

"Ruby, I can't do any of that, I am a midwife. I will make sure you and the baby are healthy."

"Pearl, I don't want a slave baby," insists Ruby. "I am not a slave-making machine; I am not going to bring babies into this world to make Bellamy rich. Pearl, I am a woman, I have feelings, and I want to love a man, not just lay with him to have a child for the master.

"Sam is walking around with the biggest grin on his face. Ben gave him a piece of silver and me red satin for a dress. Ben intends to make me have a child, have a family and accept my lot in life as a slave. I will not do it."

"Ruby, you have to make the best of this situation. I know how you must feel, but I cannot help you. I can't do anything to put your life or that of the baby's in danger. When was the last time you and Sam were together, you know what I mean?" I ask. "When did you see your flowers last?"

"Two months or so, I don't know. I've been sick and I just know there is a baby in here," pointing to her belly.

"Doesn't add up, Ruby, were you late when you married Sam?" I inquire.

"I haven't seen my flowers since Cato was sold away. Too much sorrow in my life for my flowers to come. I prayed for my flowers to never be seen again."

"Ruby, I don't think this is Sam's baby."

"What? What are you saying?" asks a wide-eyed Ruby.

"Ruby, you are carrying Cato's child." Tears roll down Ruby's cheeks as she struggles to catch her breath. "It can't be, we always...." Then she remembers the night they were watched.

"Ruby, you still love Cato with every bit of your soul. Keep dreaming about the day you will be together again. Things are changing. The abolitionists are getting strong, even in Charleston. Think of this -- it is Cato's child."

"So tell me, Pearl, how will that make things better? Only means I will never see Cato again. Pearl, Cato and I made a vow to each other. We married ourselves in the lavender field, vowed that together or apart, neither of us would have a child unless that child was free. Wherever he is, he is governed by those vows, just as I am. I cannot have a slave child."

"Ruby, listen to yourself, this child is the result of your love for Cato." I am mystified at her behavior; this is Cato's child.

"Pearl, the love of enslaved people carries a price; to love is to put not only your body but your spirit, and eventually any child, in danger."

"But, Ruby, love and family are all that enslaved people have. Yes, we love each other, we have a child that may be sold, but we still love him, and we have another to love in its place. Our families affirm our humanity; ensure that we as a people survive to tell our story."

"But love yearns for freedom, love desires to be protected, to exist for its own reason. We love because we are human, we have children because we love ourselves and our mate, love exists for its own reason, not for the whims of the master," challenges Ruby. "It is because of my love for Cato that I cannot betray his trust. We vowed that we would never have a child that was not born free. And what kind of love is it to bring a slave into the world?"

"Ruby, all of the women in the quarters love their children."

"Yes, but every woman in the quarters has lost a part of herself each time a child produced from love is sold. Look at Maude, she went insane. Mary hardly speaks since her boys were sold. To have a slave child is to know love and misery entwined, it is bittersweet. You cannot have one without the other. Pearl, have you ever thought about what it does to the mother who loses her child or to the child who looks behind crying for the helpless mother who cannot save him?"

"Ruby, I only do what is mine to do, to help women bring children into this world. I am a midwife. Midwifery has been in my family for hundreds of years. There is nothing else for me."

"I heard it come from his own lips, Bellamy's plan is to ensure his future and the future of his children by producing slaves. If I have this child, he or she will not belong to me, but to Bellamy. I refuse to make him rich by giving him another slave child that will eventually be taken from me anyway."

I could see the anger building in her. She looked at with me with disgust. "And what would you know of love? You have never felt a man's arms around you. You have never had a child."

"My children are all of the children in the quarters, they all belong to me."

"Is that enough, Pearl? Don't you ever wish one of the children born could have been born by you?"

"I have never thought of it in that way, except for you. Ruby, I was chosen at birth to help bring children into this world. Yes, even enslaved children."

"That's fine for you, but not for me. I'd rather be dead."

"Hush, stop this crazy talk now. This is your life, girl. Accept it. You have been fighting as long as you have been born. Killed your momma trying not to be born and tried to die anyway, if Auntie Ama and I hadn't saved you. Been sulking and stubborn all your days. You never see good in anything, always off somewhere in your own world. Well, Ruby, this is your world, accept it. You have been protected by me since you were born. Without my love and protection, you would have been sold long ago. Ruby, I love you. I love you the way I would if you had come from my own body. You are my daughter."

"Well, Mother, if you love me so much, why don't you help me? Why did you try so hard to save me, Pearl? Mina says I fought not to be born."

"Oh, yes, Mina says. Your mother was dying, I had to save you."

"You played the good midwife role, save Master Ben's child at any cost."

Before I knew what was happening, my hand made a swift blow to Ruby's right cheek.

"Oh, Ruby, I am sorry, I didn't mean to...." "I grab her to my breast. "What you are saying is unfair, dearest girl. I did not let your mother die, she refused to live. I saved you and I have loved you like a daughter. How can you talk this way?" Tears flow down my cheeks.

"Pearl, Bellamy may think he owns all of me, thinks he can force me to have a slave child to grow lonely in a world without her mother or father, but remember this, he may own my body and my labor, he may force me to marry a man I do not love, but the only power I have as a woman is my womb, and that power I will not give away. I will never have a slave child." Ruby turns and walks across the street.

I do not know what will happen or when she will talk to me again. I sit and weep the bitter tears of a mother who has just lost her child.

Lavender Bouquets

Even though Ruby does not come to visit me at the sick house, I watch her come and go to the dairy. I inquire of Sam how things are. "You two must be getting along much better now. I must admit, I don't hear arguments anymore." Sam laughs and I add, "I see the candles burning late into the night."

"That's Ruby, can't get her to go to bed early. She loves that red satin cloth Master Ben gave her, been working on a special dress to wear when we present our baby. She's different now. Ruby is real quiet, but I think having the baby is settling her down. She is not so mean anymore, fixes my supper, real sweet."

"I see her going into the woods on Saturdays, is she collecting herbs?"

"She's been drying lavender, says she's going to make every woman in the quarters a lavender bouquet. I tell you she's really changed."

"Tell Ruby to come over here soon; it is time for me to see her. Miss Charlotte has asked about her."

~~~~~~~~~~~~

A pregnant Ruby surprises me this morning. She is radiant. I am so happy to see her. We hug each other tightly.

"Pearl, I am sorry for the way I talked to you and for not coming back to see you. But I have something for you. I have made one for all of the women in the village, but yours is the most special. I put the most time and work into making yours." She hands me a bouquet of dried lavender tied with a red ribbon from a basket full of little bouquets and red ribbons.

"Ruby, this is lovely, and it will make the cabin smell wonderful. I have missed you so much. Please come in and have a cup of tea with me. It will be good for you and the baby."

"Thank you. I will stop briefly but I have to deliver the rest of the bouquets."

"Ruby, I am sorry too for my words the last time we spoke. See? I knew it would all work out. Sam will be happy to have a child, and he need never know the truth. You and he can have more children. Remember, you are very lucky because Ben will never sell any of your children, and they will probably get to work in the Big House." A slight frown crosses Ruby's face, but she says nothing.

"How is that dress coming along? Sam says you work on it every night. I bet it is going to be beautiful. When can I see it?"

"It will be beautiful. It will be the most special dress that I will ever own. You'll see it soon."

Ruby drinks her tea and gets up to leave. She stops briefly in the doorway. "Pearl, I love you dearly, you have been my mother, my sister, and my protector. Know that no matter what turn my life may take, I love you."

"Ruby, don't worry, you and the baby will be fine. Remember, I am your midwife," I say smiling and anticipating the delivery. "I need you to come in next week so I can check on you and the baby. I want to make sure you are not working too hard and that you are getting the amount of food that you need to have a healthy child."

"Pearl, the baby and I will be fine, just remember that I love you."

I caress the lavender bouquet, put it on the mantle next to Abena's bag, and realize that I am weeping.

Book II
1859–1861

A Sunday Morning, 1859

I look out of my cabin door into the warm morning. The birds nesting in the trees chirp madly in the spring air. Smoke drifts from the chimneys of all the cabins. The fragrance of honeysuckle fills the air. *What a wonderful Sunday morning,* I think as my eyes study the street, just a well-worn path it is that separates the cabins on either side and stretches from the cotton fields at the rear to the vast green lawn surrounding the Big House where Master Ben and Mistress Charlotte live. Our unpainted, shabby wooden cabins, most with only one bedroom, squat behind aged oak trees that make everything soft with an illusion of graciousness. The cabins are home to the fifty or so of us African slaves on the Bellamy Plantation.

In the cabin next to mine lives Auntie Ama, the old woman who cares for the young children and raises those who are orphaned because of death or the sale of both parents. I live in one of the two rooms of the sick house where I spend my days and nights tending to slaves who are hurt or ill. It is Sunday, and there are only two sick persons hanging around; most seem to have recovered sufficiently, even Sancho. *It's amazing how Sunday can bring miraculous healings,* I think as I smile to myself. Directly across from the sick house is the cabin of the enslaved driver Sam and his new wife, Ruby.

I just stand and gaze out my window, loving the handsome hundred-year-old oak, its huge limbs draped with Spanish moss. From the top branches of this towering tree the children say they can see the cotton fields. Its roots, which extend out like tentacles, are where the children spend hours at play. Even though we are enslaved, we have a tree that says to us we are protected and kept cool, that we too live in beauty. This tree, the gathering place for us residents of the quarters, is where our social life takes place. Hand-hewn benches, made by the men on a Saturday afternoon, surround the tree; two heavy black pots simmer with our communal dinner later today. Tables laden with tantalizing rabbit and catfish stews, dandelion greens and sweet potato pone will be laid out for the picnic held after the preaching. Under the cover of these ancient branches, fiddlers play and the dancing extends well into the early morning hours. On Saturday afternoon women gather to sew or shell peas while men clean fish and skin animals caught from the creek and woods nearby as they tell boastful stories. In the pale moonlight, long after the overseer has checked the cabins to make sure all of the enslaved are asleep, this oak provides young lovers a semblance of peace and privacy. Just beyond the tree are the cabins of the house slaves and then the arbor that separates us from the free.

I hear the excited chatter of the children next door who are preparing for the Sunday stroll through the quarters' street on their way to the preaching. Their happiness on this Sunday morning warms my heart. These are my children, though not of my own body, but children that I, midwife, have brought into the world. When I see them stepping sprightly on Sunday mornings, I am proud of my work.

I step away from the window and consider each of the two dresses on the bed. I hold my favorite, the yellow one decorated with the shell buttons, up to my shoulders. *But, no, it isn't right.* I think as I study the second one and run my fingers down the front.

This is the one for today.

I slip it over my head. It fits me perfectly. The white eyelet top with full bellowing sleeves and low-cut bodice reveals a bit of my bosom. The flowing deep blue skirt cinched by a red band accentuates my tiny waist. I splash rose petal water behind my ears, on my neck, arms and bosom. I breathe in the fragrance and let out a satisfied sigh.

I smile to myself. This smart dress makes me feel pretty. It will surely catch the eye of even the Master. I twirl around, holding the tail of my dress as I admire my own beauty. I am indeed well-favored. Smooth, light-brown skin, soft green eyes, high cheekbones, a slightly broad nose, thin lips. I am solidly built, with a narrow waist and broad hips. My thick, wavy hair usually worn in two braids atop my head is swept back into a bun. Ringlets at my cheeks are accented by a white rose tucked behind my right ear.

I quickly lace my shoes as I hear the chattering of women walking up the street of the quarters. The Sunday parade is beginning.

These women, who have worn dirty, sweaty, shabby shifts as they labored in the fields, are transformed. On Sunday, this one day of rest, they are not laboring like men; they feel and look like women who revel in all their feminine glory. All week, they have been forced to give their overworked bodies unwillingly to the Master's coffers. On Saturday afternoons, they come in from the fields and begin the ritual of preparing to reclaim their womanhood. Dressing up on Sunday is a means of self-expression and the one time these enslaved women can assert their femininity.

The transformation is something to behold, I think. These women who looked ragged and slovenly, with uncombed hair and unwashed bodies and who appeared to care nothing of their appearance during the work week, become sweet-smelling beauties with neatly combed hair, clothing as closely matching that of the mistress as they can configure. On Sundays, these women wear starched, full, crisp skirts with hoops made from grapevines or tiny tree limbs. They wear fluffy sleeves, high collars and show off their colorful dresses dyed from tree barks and plants gathered from the woods.

Head rags come off on Sunday as women who had wrapped their hair in twine and covered it during the week display their curls. Some wear flowers and fancy combs in their hair, others choose to wear a Sunday bonnet or many-colored head wrap.

I breathe in the sweet fragrance that saturates the morning air. I am dazzled by the array of colors and the special touches that each woman gives herself. I laugh as I savor the sound of woman talk passing my cabin.

"Lovey, I know Joe is going to be pleased to see you today. Why, he won't want to go back yonda to his plantation. Don't git that man in no trouble," teases Annie.

"Don't you say nuttin' 'bout me. Who you takin' dat head rag off fo' and showin' dem curls of yors fo'? You are lookin' right pretty yorself today," says Lovey as she touches Annie's curls.

"How did you git dat red to be so pretty?" asks Polly of Mary. "I try and try and it don't ever come out right."

"Girl, you know what I do, I adds me a bucket of dat chamber lye. Does the trick ev'ry time," laughs Mary.

"Good morning, Cousin Pearl, you are looking right pretty this morning." A compliment from Violet, the best-dressed women in the quarters, is indeed a compliment. She is one who exchanges produce from her garden and homespun goods for decorative cloth that she spends endless evenings making into fine dresses for Sunday.

"Well, Violet, you have outdone yourself today," I say. "That yellow is your color. And none of us can match the fullness of your skirt today."

Many of the younger women have been delivered by me. They love to receive the generous compliments that I give as they pass. "Why, Rosa," I exclaim, "what beautiful buttons you are wearing this morning! Did you make them yourself?"

"Yes, Ma'am, Cousin Pearl. And what do you think of my necklace?"

"It is as beautiful as you!"

"My, don't you look pretty this morning, little Patsy! What a pretty blue dress."

"Mama worked real hard every night to make it for me.

In their Sunday dress, the girls and women who pass along the street are pleased with themselves, self-assured and confident in their beauty. In fact, they don't just walk past, they strut all the way down the street of the quarters to the Master's yard where the service is held. I take great pleasure in watching the procession and laugh to myself when the girls pass in their Sunday finery walking barefoot. They are so particular about their shoes that they sling them over their shoulders and put them on when they reach the grass of the Big House.

"That's right, don't get those shoes dirty," I tease.

"Come on now, Cousin Pearl, time for you to join us. Almost time for the preachin' to start."

"You go right ahead, I am on my way." I check on the two patients and give them each a cup of tea. "I won't be gone long. You will be okay until I return," I tell them.

Suddenly, the splendor and peace of Sunday morning is shattered by piercing screams and shrieks. I step outside my doorway and lean as far as I can to see what is happening, but I can only hear the commotion. I race down the steps and follow the others heading toward the source of the tumult. All I can see are faces and fingers pointing upward, like Jesus himself had descended upon the big oak tree. My heart is pounding as I run as fast as I can. Perhaps someone is hurt or sick. No preaching for me today, I think. But as I get closer, I can't believe my eyes. Women are passed out on the ground and some are beating their breasts and burying their faces in their hands, giving no regard to their nice garments being dirtied. I shield my eyes as I inch closer. The Sunday parade has ended in an orgy of grief under the giant oak tree, the source of joy and comfort for the people of the quarters.

The women wearing harried wild expressions look up at the tree as they claw at their clothing or sit rocking and moaning on the ground. Children cry and men stare in shock.

What can this be? What horror has befallen?
With each step I take, my body now trembles and
my heart feels as though it will burst from my chest. I
clasp my hands over my ears to block the sounds of
crying and screaming. I creep closer. I lift my head
upward slowly, reluctantly, and then I squeeze my
eyes tightly shut.

I hold my head in my hands and shake it in
denial as I hear terrible wails gush from my mouth.
"No! No! No! This cannot be! Oh, God, what have
I done?" Gasping for air, I sink, my legs weaken, and
dizziness overcomes me. I slide to the ground,
whimpering and muttering unintelligible words of
contrition.

The Sinful Act

I struggle to lift my body and to open my unbelieving eyes. The crate on which she had stood to fasten the noose has been kicked aside. This is not dream, it is fact. Here hanging above me, her feet almost touching my head is Ruby, dressed in a radiant red satin dress, a daisy intertwined in her neatly braided hair, polished black shoes gleaming in the sunlight. Her peaceful face embraces a slight smile. Ruby, the child that I brought into the world, had fought to keep alive and loved as though she were my own daughter, has taken her life and that of her unborn child.

"Ruby, why? Ruby, we could have found a way. Oh, Ruby."

As my words fall upon her un–hearing ears, Sam, Ruby's husband, grumbling and cussing, forces himself through the throng that silently and obediently parts to make way for the most privileged slave among us. He yells his cusses as he stomps through the gathering crowd. "Why are you niggas making all this noise? What's wrong with you niggas? What are you niggas looking at?" When he finally looks up, an awful grimace comes over his face.

"What the hell?" His eyes widen with terror, his jaw drops and an ugly grunt explodes from his mouth. He falls to the ground sobbing uncontrollably, a sight no one ever thought they'd see from a man who has always been mean.

The crowd inches back, still in silence. Only Sam and I remain beneath the corpse. The sounds of the wind, the birds and nature's creatures seem frivolous within the dense quiet of the people and the tragedy hanging from the tree.

~~~~~~~~~~~~~~~~

The Big House is a two story white structure with four columns in front, black shutters on the windows, and verandas that encircle from front to back. When the weather permits, after the minister finishes the service for the family and neighbors inside, he delivers a message of salvation in the hereafter for the slaves from the second-story veranda. We bring coverings to sit on the lawn below.

The family service over, Master Ben directs the minister to the veranda and is making him comfortable. He has ignored what he thought was screaming and crying, but now that he can hear it better, he is perturbed when he sees not one slave on the lawn for the sermon.

"Pastor, make yourself comfortable, I'll be right back," says the Master. "Let me see what's keeping these niggas." He rushes down the stairs, grabs a riding whip from the umbrella stand beside the door and strides out. From his vantage point, Master Ben can see the crowd under the large oak tree. He becomes more and more irritated as he walks briskly to the group.

"What you niggas waiting for? The preacher is here. Come on now!" He pushes his way through the grief-struck people, swinging the whip as he goes, hitting women and children randomly. Everyone moves away from him, those hit cringe but refuse to cry out. Suddenly, he stops in his tracks, his face and neck turning splotchy red as his mouth hangs open. After his brief minute of shock, we can see the magnitude of the situation dawning upon him. His manner changes abruptly. He again tears through the crowd, hitting slaves more fiercely with his whip.

"Get outta here! Go to the preaching!" he yells. "Get away from this sinful scene. This wench is going to hell for sure!" He has his back to Ruby now and yells out at us, "Save yourselves, get up there to the house now."

Women ruin their dresses as they crawl across the grass, some trip over others, all of them try to get away from the Master. Men grab the hands of crying children and run toward the Big House. Still in a state of shock I watch the panicked scene and then swivel to look briefly into the hateful eyes of Master Ben. As I crawl away toward the Big House lawn I hear him beating Sam upon the head with his crop and yelling at him.

"Bury her. Now!"

I am horrified. I gasp and cover my mouth.

"Take her somewhere in the woods," he yells. "And you let nobody, I mean nobody, know where. I want no sign of her around when these niggas get out of service."

I glance back to see Sam lifting the stiff body. He looks down into her face and begins to weep again. Hunched with her weight and his grief, he slowly carries Ruby toward the woods.

The Master strides angrily back to the Big House and whispers into the ear of the minister whose face and neck redden. He jumps up staring wild-eyed at the black faces dragging themselves onto the lawn. He clears his throat, wipes his brow and swivels his head to take in all of them, the still weeping, stooped humans before him. Glaring across the black mass and without looking at his Bible, he begins. "The Bible says that to take one's own life is a sin!" he screams. "Says it right here in Job 1:21 that God is the giver of life. He gives and he takes away." He waves his arm and points his finger out toward the oak tree. His deeply red face reddens even more, and I think he might explode. He speaks hysterically, condemning, as usual. "Satan is here hiding in the quarters, calling you to sin. It is Satan that steered this wicked woman to commit such a terrible sin against God and her Master. She killed the innocent child that God had given her, a blessed child that belonged to Bellamy plantation, and she has abandoned her grieving husband."

The minister pauses, waiting in vain for "amens" from the heads bowed in silence or staring blank-eyed into the nothing. He shakes his head in stern disapproval. "It is not up to us to rebel against the will of God, even when the reasons may seem a mystery to us. Scripture says that God has ordained the black man to serve. We cannot question God or his wisdom. And we must serve with love and willingness in our hearts."

If any of us look at him it is through the slits of our eyes full of tears.

"Y'all know that what she did was wrong. That wicked soul will never be able to look upon the face of Jesus in heaven. She committed a sinful act, an act of blasphemy, from which she cannot repent. Taking one's own life is forbidden by the fifth commandment, Thou shalt not kill! When she put that rope around her neck, she committed two murders, self-murder and the murder of that innocent child. She had no authority to commit such an awful act."

Glassy eyes stare straight ahead and there are again no responses to him. I hear what he says but do not acknowledge it or him. Like the other women of the quarters, I am deep in shock intermingled with practical thoughts. *Who will bring Ruby to the sick house so that her body can be washed? Who will help with the delicate, loving and necessary task of preparing and dressing Ruby for burial? What will the women take from her cabin to decorate her grave?*

The crowd shifts restlessly when the preacher says, "Your life is the property of God and the property of your Master. Don't let her sin put ideas into your head about escaping your earthly life.

Remember, servants, honor and obey your Master so that you will rejoice in your heavenly home. That poor wench will burn forever in hell for that dreadful act!"

As soon as the preaching stops we move as one, silent, across the lawn and back down the street of the quarters. As we trudge through a new hell, we have other things besides heaven on our minds. There will be no picnic. Tonight, we will give Ruby the best funeral that we can.

When they do not see Ruby's body hanging from the tree, several of the men hurry to Sam's cabin.

"Where de body, Sam? We come to git it for de women to wash."

"She ain't here, buried already. Massa said she don't deserve no funeral." Sam sits on his floor, his whole body shaking.

"How you gon bury Ruby so fast? Is you crazy, man?"

"That's the way Massa want it."

"What? Ain't righ! Dat po girl deserve a funeral."

"Says he don't want no niggas to get ideas and think they get a decent Christian burial when they commit a sin against God. He tells me 'Get up!

Get up!' He grabs me by the collar and forces me to stand. He yells, 'Get this wench down!' I grabbed the crate Ruby stood on. I had to hold her while Massa cut her down. I had to hold my Ruby's stiff body to my chest while he sawed at the rope with his sword. She was stiff 'n hard." Sam is trembling so fiercely, his teeth chatter. The men back away. Sam babbles on.

When they finally come out, single file, Sally shouts out angrily, "Where's Ruby?"

"Sam say she bury already," answers one of the men.

"That can't be, you fools. Ruby got to have a funeral."

"Massa don' think so."

"But where she bury? We can go there."

"Sam say Massa don' wont nobody messin' wit her grave; it hid in de woods."

The fact of the unbelievable hiding of Ruby's body settles over the quarters like a thick fog. I watch the crowd split into little groups whispering and confused as they wander around, pointless and scared. Soon enough, anger replaces tears. The shock of the act has been absorbed. Loud gasps are heard as women and men begin to shake their heads and grumble louder.

"Massa makin' a big mistake now. Can't have Ruby spirit wandrin' all 'roun the quarters causin' trouble," warns Hannah.

"Dat girl was trouble enough when she livin', she gon be worse now, "echoes Susie.

A young pregnant slave wearing a red satin dress with a daisy in her hair has just gained freedom for herself and her child, I think woefully. *This will be a Sunday that nobody in the quarters will ever forget.* I have a sudden untoward thought: *The Master, too, will lament this day.*

I struggle back to the sick house, peer at the questioning eyes of the sick who have surely heard the commotion through the open window, but I am unable to care for their needs and barely get it out that Ruby has hung herself. I ask Auntie Ama to summon Lizzie and Priscilla to come attend the sick. The girls, still wearing their Sunday dresses, appear with reddened eyes and drawn faces.

Lizzie says, "Cousin Pearl, we will take care to the sick. You res' now."

I feel faint, can barely catch my breath, and the tears flow without end. As soon as I lie down and close my eyes, the image of Ruby hanging from the oak tree tears into my mind. I am consumed with her red satin dress, knowing how the whole scene was designed perfectly by her. I feel the fire of her emotions, her passion, and her defiance. A red satin dress is usually worn only by the mistress as a symbol of her status and power. Bellamy's gift of the red satin material to Sam for Ruby was to symbolize his power over her, her obedience and submission to him through Sam by having what he believed would be one of many children the couple would bear for the plantation. Ruby had outwitted Bellamy. The red satin dress she had so painstakingly made was a demonstration of her power to fulfill her vow to never have a slave child.

I admire her courage, but her act gives me no solace. My grief is unbearable. It drills a hole in my insides that leaves only a wound. She was more special to me than any other child I brought into the world. I love her like a daughter. *How can she be gone?*

I finally drift off to sleep but jerk awake by visions of Ruby hanging from the tree. The scene gnaws at the back of my mind. Night has come, but I know that sleep will not stay with me, so I pull my weary body from the bed, change out of my once pretty dress into my nightshirt and stumble through the darkness to the door, careful not to wake the sick. l step outside and a cool breeze crosses my face.

Shoeless, I navigate through the dark night toward the tree. It is pitch black except for the light of a candle shining through Sam's open window. *Well, Ruby is denying both of us peace.*

As I approach the tree, a cold shiver goes through me and I trip over one of the roots and fall. I crawl along the roots, putting my hands out to touch the ancient trunk. I place my back tight up against it and slide down until I am sitting on the root just below where Ruby hung, my mind a blank. I hope to sleep until I hear the bell calling the field hands.

But rather than being lulled to sleep, I am once again awash in ugly scenes. Hot, bitter tears run down my cheeks. I see images of Ruby's mother lying in a pool of blood below the tree as Ruby hangs from a branch above wearing the red satin dress. For the first time, I question my role as midwife. Words I do not expect pour from my mouth.

"Now you and your mother are gone. What kind of midwife am I? What cruel turn of fate has befallen me? How is it possible that I lost both you and your mother?" I quiet my voice but my mind will not still. *I have been a midwife since I was a mere girl. My grandmother Abena, who raised me, said it was my calling, that midwives and healing women had been in my family for generations.*

My Abena had been the midwife and nurse for the quarters as long as I knew. At ten years of age, even before I had seen my flowers, I accompanied Granny Abena when babies had to be delivered in the quarters. "Aunt" and "Granny" are the titles given to the women who are midwives and nurses, but because of my young age, everyone in the quarters calls me "Cousin" or "Sister" Pearl, as a sign of respect for my position. I remember well my apprenticeship as a midwife.

"Get the water boiling, chile, "Granny Abena ordered. "While the water boils, make the pallet."

"Yes, Ma'am." I always answered obediently.

When it was time for the birth, I was called close to observe Granny's skilled performance.

"See, now just keep rubbing her stomach like this."

"Say some soothing things to the mother to make it easier."

"Chile, I forgot, get the knife and put it under the bed to help cut the pains."

"Look here, Pearl, this baby is comin'!" She pulled me closer. "See that head peakin' now? "That's called crownin'."

When I wasn't attending births, I was cutting and sewing materials for the mothers, finding herbs for healing teas, and caring for patients at the sick house. I was barely into my teen years when the awesome task of becoming midwife and nurse for the enslaved community was thrust upon me because Granny Abena died. Now at 30 years of age, I have settled into the role that has given me a sense of identity and esteem within the enslaved community. But Ruby's suicide has made me question everything I have known or thought about myself. Now I wonder. *Was I given the gift of being a midwife? Or is it a curse?*

Where Is Ruby?

There is a belief in the quarters that the spirit of the dead stays around for three days before it leaves for eternal rest. What everyone in the quarters fears is that if Ruby's grave is not found, she will have no peace and remain a wandering spirit to commit mischief.

I have been awake all night and have seen the comings and goings of women into the woods in search of Ruby's body. Now those dark, desperately tired and bent bodies pour out of cabins to collect work tools. The men and women march separately, weary and broken in their thoughts and actions. There is only the dark sky, somber silence, and the sound of brogans slicing through the grass. Today, there is a different heaviness in the air. The quarters carry more than their hoes on tired shoulders; they carry emotional and spiritual fears. I know the women are exhausted. In shifts, they have spent the better part of the night in search of Ruby but to no avail. Their quick glances pronounce their fear. As they pass, I hear their pleadings.

"Oh, God, please help us find dat Ruby."

"We mus' find Ruby 'n gib her a right burial or her spirit will upset de quarters somethin' terrible."

"Where did he put our Ruby?" they whisper.

"God know she got to be here somewhere, but no sign of de grave."

"We gots to find her. God know dat chile be trouble when she livin'; quarters don't need no trouble from her dead," warns Susie.

"Dat rat may hab throw her in de ribber, do anyting Massa say."

Several of the women agree to search the riverbank the next day.

For an entire week, after laboring in the fields, the women take turns in the woods looking for herbs or some pretense, but they find no grave. In the evenings, the harried and weary men pretend to hunt or fish while they too search for Ruby's grave.

The Oak Tree – Abomination

It has been a week now, and there is no sign of Ruby's grave. With no choice but to resign themselves, the people of the quarters once again try to accept a fate that has befallen them. It is nigh impossible this time. As they often do on Saturday afternoon, the women sit under the big oak tree to shell peas, exchange vegetables from gardens, and socialize. Today, the men go one last time searching; the women sit under the tree, their eyes drifting up to the limb from which Ruby hung herself.

"Dat chile was tryin' to tell us sum ting," says old blind Mina, nodding her head as if she is privy to a secret. This is her usual way, so no one pays her much mind.

"Mina born wid a caul over her, maybe she seen Ruby, "whispers Patsy with a smirk.

On Saturday night, when the men return, the mood of those gathered under the oak tree changes dramatically. They have decided they will do what little they can. l sit on my stoop and listen to the quarters change from resignation to respect for the dead. Joe looks up at the limb on which Ruby hung and proclaims, "Ruby sho free now, ain't no slave no more." The others nod in agreement. As the night wears on, the quarters celebrate Ruby in story and song.

"Dat one stubborn baby. Pearl had to struggle to git her out. Din't want to be born no slave," says Hannah.

Aunt Ama remembers with a smile on her face. "She jus' herself, not like the udder chillen."

"'Member when she wander off the men had to find her?" pipes Sally. "Dere she was, jus' sittin' outside dere wid Mina, not a worry in dis worl'." They all laugh, but the loudest laughs are reserved for Ruby's pretending to have the "nigga disease" that kept Bo from having her. "Got her thrown outta the Big House, however much old Bo wanted dat sweet brown sugar." The crowd guffaws and pounds tables in laughter.

I realize how much they admired the young girl who refused to accept being a slave. There are some with spirits that cannot be bound, like the saying from the old people that if a baby dies before the ninth day, it is because the spirit doesn't want to stay here in the hell of slavery. Some of us endure, others adopt little ways to rebel, but those with spirits like Ruby cannot pretend or wear a mask. They run away countless times until they are successful, they fight back, they allow themselves to be killed to deny the master a profit from them, or like Ruby, they kill themselves. Those who do this make the biggest statement, choosing death over bondage. By any means necessary, they will be free.

From the veranda of the Big House Master Ben watches the scene below. He calls to Miss Charlotte. "What are the niggas up to? Looks like they are having some kind of celebration under the tree where that wench hung herself. I'll take care of that situation, I promise."

~~~~~~~~~~~~~

Master Bellamy keeps his promise on Sunday. We wait, grudgingly, to hear Rev. Brian's preaching for the quarters. This morning his mien is determined and serious. He wipes his crimson forehead and under his several chins, clears his throat and begins to preach to us, the slave flock.

"God is watching you today," he intones. "Every man, woman, and child of you. He is looking into your hearts and he can see the difference between the believers and the non-believers. He knows which ones of you see that suicide as an abomination. That taking one's life, depriving his master of the service that God has required from the descendants of Ham is an awful sin." Some women lower their heads and twist their lips in pure disdain. The less brave pretend to agree by bobbing their heads with the preacher.

"On yesterday, you turned out in celebration at the site of this most grievous sin. You ate, laughed, and jested under the very limb on which the greatest sin that one can commit was carried out. What do you think God was thinking of your turning your face from his laws? That girl and that tree are abominations. That tree is like the snake that tempted Adam. And like Adam was cast from the kingdom, the tree upon which that sin was committed must be cast from this place. To protect you from the Devil's sinful callings, the tree must be destroyed, leaf, branch, and root. Is this understood? You will no longer gather in that sinful spot. Know that this action is taken for your own eternal good, so that you will never be tempted to commit such an act against God and Master."

We are struck dumb.

Then Master Ben stands tall, takes a deep breath and issues the decree. "There is no gathering in the quarters today. When the preaching is done, return to your cabins, get on your knees and ask

God's forgiveness for your sins. Tomorrow after you return from the fields, every man is to show up at the sinful tree, and you are to cut and hack each day after work until every sign of the tree is gone. Then you will take ropes, chains, and a mule to pull the root from the ground. The women are to cut the limbs into firewood and the children are to carry the firewood to the woodhouse. Everyone in the quarters must bear the burden for the terrible sin of suicide. That sinful woman whose name God will not allow me to call committed the ultimate act of selfishness. She had no love in her heart for the precious life that she carried. No woman with human motherly instincts would perform such an act."

~~~~~~~~~~~~~~~~

This Sunday, only one week later, the tree is gone. The men, women, and children work all week as they were told. The inhabitants of the quarters wear strained, anxious looks. There is no place to gather. They refuse to look at the hole where the tree was. They are at loose ends, confused, wary. Percy notices and forces songs in the fields; the meaning of the words he does not understand.

"Oh woe on we, wandering spirit have pity on us, be patient, Oh woe on we." The women sing the refrain over and over. When they pat their feet in a rhythmic step and hoe to the rhythm, Percy thinks this is a good sign and that things are getting back to normal in the quarters. Sam, now constantly drinking and reeking of liquor each day, has become confused and fearful. "Cut out that noise, you hear, shut up." Percy, being the overseer, tells Sam to shut up and demands that the women continue to sing.

The quarters is bound in a tight knot, ready for more disaster at any minute, both grieving and angry. Everyone is on edge, sleepless nights long, daybreak arriving too soon. Gardens go to weeds, women barely have energy to prepare meals. There is no extra wild meat or fish to supplement. Husbands yell and hit wives, mothers yell and hit children. Minds are occupied with only one thing, finding Ruby's grave and avoiding more disaster they expect soon to befall them from the Master. The stress is undoing the quarters but there is more to come.

Old blind Mina summons the women to gather at Auntie Ama's cabin after lights are out and Percy has checked the cabins. I am anxious and unsure of what will come from the old woman's mouth. I, like the others, obey and listen intently as she begins.

"Ruby come to me last night in a dream, tol' me to warn you a things to come. Things gonna be bad in the quarters -- death, sickness, sadness. Her spirit jus wandrin'. We gots to find her grave 'n pray her across. Won't be no peace in the quarters until dat girl at peace."

Sally lets out a loud sigh.

"What we gon' do?" pleads Sarah. "How we gon' find Ruby's grave? We ain't had time to look cuz a dat tree. I so tired, I kin hardly stan'."

"But we mus' try, we gots to find dat grave."

Women wring their hands and shuffle their feet. Some weep. "Ruby know we love her, we tryin' to find her."

Darkness Falls Upon the Quarters

Dan

Ruby's cloud of darkness begins to descend upon the quarters today. First, the accidents: Dan, a hearty, strapping man, one of Bellamy's most trusted, is returning from taking a load of cotton bales to Charleston for sale, when some five miles from the plantation the horses rear; he tries to keep control, but they overturn the wagon, crushing him. It is midnight before patty rollers discover the overturned wagon and bring him to the plantation. I work feverishly to clean and take care of Dan's wounds, but his legs are crushed. Bellamy calls in Dr. Smith who gives the bad news. Dan's legs will have to be amputated; he will never walk again.

Dan, despite his pain, motions me to come by his cot. I press my ear to his mouth. He tells me a story that makes me wince. I take a deep breath and ask if he is sure of the details.

"I know what spooked the horses, it was her."

"Her who?"

"It was Ruby. She was standin' in the middle a de road, wearin' dat red dress. I see her clear as day.

Dere was light roun' her, skeered the horses half to death. I cain't hol' onto 'em."

"Are you sure you saw Ruby?" I ask.

"Sister Pearl, I ain't a liar and I ain't crazy, I knows when I sees sumtin', 'n I saw Ruby."

"I don't think you are lying or crazy, this is just so unbelievable," I say. Slowly I lift myself from beside his pallet. *Can Mina be right? Can this be true?* I wonder. The preacher teaches us the Christian way and says when we die we go to heaven or hell and Ruby is surely in hell. But Mina believes in the African way, says, "If spirits aren't helped to cross over, they bodder de livin'."

Thomas

The very next day, Thomas gets kicked by a mare he has worked with for years. When the men bring him to the sick house, I show them to a pallet. Thomas, wide-eyed, lies gasping for air, trying to speak. "Raised her from a colt. Kicked me so hard, I think she broke my ribs."

I calm him down. "Thomas, I will take good care of you. You will be fine. Just try to relax. We need to take your shirt off." I call one of the men to help me. Thomas grabs me by the shoulder and pulls me close to his ear. "It was her, it was her."

"What her are you talking about?" I ask, already knowing the answer.

In a halting, labored breath, he whispers," It Ruby. She do sometin' to Lucy, and so dat mare rear up 'n kick me. Oh, Cousin Pearl, I cain't breathe. Please hep me."

"Please, Joe, get Master Bellamy, Thomas needs a doctor. Quick."

While Joe races to the Big House, I make a mist to help him breathe. I give him healing tea, but by the time the doctor arrives, Thomas is spitting up blood and dies soon after.

I weep and beat my forehead and then I scream, "Ruby, why are you doing this? What have these poor people done to you? They are just slaves, like you were. They live terrible lives of bondage and backbreaking work. Why are you punishing them more?" As I ask the question, Mina appears.

"May I come in, Aunt Pearl?" *I always feel like she is mocking me when she calls me 'Aunt' like I am an imposter, not quite up to the work as Granny Abena had been.*

"Yes, please come in, Auntie Mina."

"Seems like de sick house be busy dese days. What you think de matter?"

Sassily, I answer the old woman, even though I know better than to talk to an elder in a disrespectful way. "Perhaps you know better than I."

The old woman smiles. "I just heard you screamin' at Ruby askin' her why she hurtin' de people in de quarters. Maybe she tryin' to send dem a message."

"Then what is the message? Tell me, please, I need to know how many more bloody and suffering people I will be called upon to treat."

"Now, don' you git sassy wid me, girl. De darkness only jus' begin. Dey got to hear de message, 'n when dey do, Ruby be okay." The old woman turns away and leaves, half-smiling. She looks back at me. "Mebbe you aks Ruby to comes to you in a dream, tell you what she want, then you know."

Ralph and Mary

Ralph is a chestnut-brown, tall, broad-shouldered man. His eyes light up when he smiles. He is one of Bellamy's best and most honest hands. Ralph's pride in his stature in Bellamy's eyes is evident in his wide-toothed smile whenever he is given the task of getting supplies or ferrying Bellamy slaves to nearby plantations for visits. Ralph's wife Mary is as diminutive as Ralph is a giant of a man. A tiny women with a narrow brown face and close-set eyes, she has been paired by Bellamy with Ralph for almost a decade now. She has come to love him and the six children that they have together.

Ralph takes the wagon to Charleston to pick up a series of family portraits and get supplies. He loads the wagon, carefully packing the portraits, and heads back to Bellamy plantation. It is nearly dark, so he chirrups the horses to move along. In the middle of the road, he sees a woman dressed in red. He thinks, *She look like Ruby. But dis cain't be. Ruby dead.* He is so afraid that he blacks out. When he opens his eyes, he is surrounded by patty rollers.

"Get up, nigga, what the hell happened here?"

"I don' know, Massa, I jis'...." They pull him from under the wagon.

"Now get up, nigga," they yell.

"Massa, I cain't stand up, no feelin' in ma legs."

The paddy rollers throw him over the saddle of one of their horses and bring him to Bellamy plantation. I am barely asleep when the banging on the door awakens me. I pull a quilt around me and open up to see a bloody Ralph, unable to stand on his own.

"He's in bad shape, I'll tell Bellamy that he better call Dr. Smith," says one of the paddy rollers.

"Lay him here," I say as I gently start to remove his shirt.

"Lizzie, get up quick, heat some water and get some cloths," I say to the sleepy girl. She moves slowly to the fireplace.

"Hurry up, Ralph is hurt pretty bad."

The poor man is as frantic as he is injured. When Lizzie returns with the basin of water I begin to clean his wounds.

"Easy, Ralph. I am going to have to cut your pants away from your legs, it will be alright," I caution.

"Don' feel nuttin, Cousin Pearl. Is I, is I gon' to be able to walk? Is I gon' be lame?" Tears pour from his eyes.

I send Lizzie to get Mary. She enters the sick house with a look of quiet resolve, not shock, on her face.

She turns to me and says, "I not able to sleep. It not like Ralph be gon' 'til dark. He nebber dis late."

Mary looks at Ralph lying on the pallet, bends over him and strokes his face.

"It was her, it was Ruby," he says frantically to his wife. "She tryin' to tell us somting. Oh, Lord, what we gon do?"

I stand back and frown as the familiar words come from Mary's mouth. "She ain't gon leave us alone 'til we finds her and sends her home proper." She pats Ralph's shoulder.

"Ralph had a strange dream a few nights ago," Mary says softly. "One that made 'im sit straight up in bed, sweatin' 'n shakin'. He repeat ober 'n ober dat he seen Ruby in de middle of de road, beckon' him to her. 'Mary,' he say to me, 'I try but I caint turn de horses 'roun. I scared. Ebbybody say you ain't ebber suppose to go wit no dead folk. Dey take you into dere worl'."

Ralph is sweating heavily and weeping outright now. "I don' 'member nuttin', ebbyting jus' go dark." Mary holds her dear Ralph in her arms as tightly as she can. "I loves you 'n ebbyting be alright," she says.

Chills go through me as I hear Mary's story and watch her with her husband. *What next? Each time I close my eyes, I see you hanging from the tree, softly swaying in the wind. Ruby, you are still here aren't you?*

203

Simon

I think I have seen the worst, but the accidents escalate. This time it is Simon with shreds of bloody skin hanging from broken bones unrecognizable as a human hand. The poor man shrieks in pain, and for a moment I am overwhelmed, actually paralyzed by the scene in front of me. I catch my breath and guide him to a clean cot. I rub his forehead and try to soothe him. I whispered into his ear, "I will help you," but he continues to scream. Lizzie brings the bowl of warm water, fresh herbs, and clean cloths.

"Lizzie, you are doing a fine job, you have learned so quickly," I reassure her, relieved to have help. Lizzie took over the responsibilities of helping me in the sick house when Ruby married Sam and was assigned to the dairy, but her face is ashen.

I gently place Simon's semblance of a hand in the water, he screams. "I understand," I say softly. He raises his sad eyes and looks directly into mine and faints. For hours, I work to guide pieces of skin to their proper place on the bones of his fingers. Master Ben calls in Dr. Smith who does the unthinkable – he amputates Simon's hand above the wrist. I make a soothing tonic of whiskey and herbs; Simon sips weakly and falls to sleep.

This morning, I clean the stub at the end of Simon's arm and inquire as to what caused the accident. As he sips tea and eats a corn pone, he relays another familiar story.

"Cousin Pearl, I loadin' de bolls into de gin when I hear a wommin call my name -- 'Simon,' clear as day. I look roun fo her 'n when I do, my han' gits caught in de cylinder. James was turnin' de cylinder fast like we do, tryin' to make our quota for de day, don' wan no hittin' from Percy. James don' know my hand in dere. Dem spikes gnawin' on my hand like some wild animal. I scream but it too late for James to stop turnin'. When Percy see us stop, he come ober cussin' sumting terrible. When James stop de gin, we hab to take it all apart 'fo I can git my han' out. Ain't nebber in life had no pain like dat, worse than a lashin'. I nebber not pay attention b'fo, nebber, but dat woman, she call 'Simon' so soft. To't I knew de wommin's voice, but when I look 'roun, ain't nobody dere 'n my hand all caught up in de cylinder. Now I got one han', ain't worth much to Massa no more, guess he probably sell me for little or nuttin' to de firs' specoolator come 'long." Tears pour down Simon's face. I wipe them and hold a cup of tea to his lips. The great fear of all slaves is being sold away from family. This is the eternal emotional threat.

I curse Eli Whitney for what Master Ben calls the great savings of a lifetime. Two men can do in a few hours what it used to take four or five slaves ten hours to do. I remember when Bellamy purchased the gin, bought more slaves as well to plant more cotton. Cotton makes him rich, as those dark, bent souls labor from sun-up to sundown. I treat those swollen, aching, and deformed bodies as best I can. Now this, a man dead, one will never walk again, and another with one hand. *What horror will befall the quarters next?*

Juba

I am finishing feeding broth to Simon when the men rush into the sick house carrying Juba, the fourteen-year-old son of John and Emma. "I tink he dead fo sure," says one of the men. "Storm comin' 'n we all head out of de fiel', lightnin' bad when he start runnin' toward de big tree and talkin' all crazy. Say. 'She callin' me!' We don' see nobody nowhere. I calls to 'im to get outta de field and come wid us, but he won' listen, jus' keep yellin' 'She callin' me!'"

I look down at the young handsome brown face, thick eyebrows, full lips, a face at peace, and I know he is dead. He has been struck by lightning.

"The mysterious woman again?" I ask the men. They nod.

"Did Juba say how the woman looked?"

"No, Cousin Pearl, jus' kept goin' to de tree," one says.

I whisper to Ruby, "Was it you again? What are you trying to tell us?"

I am worried, I am confused. There are always accidents taking place on the plantation, some self-inflicted to avoid work and get needed rest for a few days. Those I smile at, treat, and do not give their secret away. Percy comes soon enough to rouse them and take them back to work. Sometimes I do wonder about the mindset of those who injure themselves to avoid work. How they must hate toiling daybreak to sundown for the benefit of another, never to share in the profits of their labor. Each day must be its own special hell; but Rev. Brian says hell is only for those who disobey their masters or commit suicide. I frown and shake my head, wearily pushing away the reverend and his stories.

Ruby, I ask, *is the thought of bringing a life into the world condemned to bondage an unspeakable and unthinkable evil?*

I begin to reflect upon evil: Is it a greater evil to protect an innocent spirit from the hell of slavery, or to bring a child into the world and condemn him or her to slavery? Is slavery itself a sin? The preacher says blacks are being punished for the sins of Canaan, but did God say that? Why is it not a sin for a master to kill a slave, but for a slave to kill herself? *Ruby, help me understand. What message did you try to leave us? What message are you trying to give us now? I beg you, come to me in a dream, speak to me, let me hear your sweet voice.*

You asked me once if I ever loved a man, if I ever wanted to have a husband, to have a child of my own. I was chosen to be the midwife; I had no time for love or for a husband, but I did have a child, not of my body but of my heart, and she is you. I grieve for you the way the mothers of the quarters grieve when their children die, are sold away from them, or they from their children. I know that I did not always understand you, appreciate your difference, how you could never see yourself as a slave though Bellamy owned you like the rest of us. Even as you were bound to a small circle of life, you created a world of your own, outside the darkness of bondage. They could never get inside your spirit. Your body may have been owned, but never your spirit, and if you had your way, the night you were born and I fought for your life, you would have never tasted the bitter brew of slavery, but I saved you, maybe as much for myself as for you. You see, this midwife would never have known the fulfillment of loving a child I considered my own, not without you. Ruby, thank you for staying this long with me, you did not deserve the life I saved you for, please forgive me, but know that I loved you and still love you dearly. Come to me.

~~~~~~~~~~~~~~~

Ruby

Last night Ruby came to me in a dream. She and I sat on the lush green grass near the lavender field, which she loved. We did not talk. She picked a sprig of lavender and placed it in my hair. I touched her hand and held it there for a moment. She walked away, turned back to me once, and she smiled.

Today, I leave Lizzie in charge of the sick house and spend the day watching the enslaved children. I walk next door to visit Granny as she and some of the eight- and nine-year-old girls tend the babies. I look into the faces of the tiny ones, all of whom I helped to bring into this world. I watch them crawl around on the dirt floor, put dirty fingers in their mouths. I watch them raise their little arms to signal that they want to be picked up. I watch them take their spoons and eat buttermilk and corn bread from the trough in the yard. I watch harried mothers hurry to Granny's to feed hungry babies after working all day in the fields, watch as babies' dark eyes look directly into the eyes of their life giver. *Do they miss the mother's touch? Do their little hearts sink each time she goes away?* I watch the little ones at play, and the slightly older pulling weeds and picking up trash on the plantation. *No childhood, only work,* I think. And like Ruby, if they are sent to play with the white children of the owner, the cruel shock will come. They will soon enough realize that they and their playmates are not friends but young Massa and slave. I remember how Ruby became physically ill at the thought of calling her little friend Bo 'Master'. She knew from childhood that she did not belong in the world of men whose greed and need to feel superior assigned her, a child of Africa, to the degradation and violence of bondage.

The Fevers

The accidents cease and the fevers begin.

I step outside to catch my breath from the stifling air inside the sick house. A gentle breeze clears the sweat and sour smells from my nostrils. I turn toward the rows of cabins to my left, tiny houses of man, woman, and child all suffering from the misery that is slavery. And something as powerful as slavery is adding to it, holding the quarters in a different kind of bondage.

I lift my head toward heaven with tears wanting to fall. I hold them back as I say out loud to God, "Why are you making these poor people suffer even more, what do you require of them?" Bodies are whipped, brutalized, worked to death, and now we are stricken with an illness that neither the doctor nor I can cure. Please help me to know how to help them."

As the words leave my lips, I hear footsteps dragging along the road from the direction of the Big House. Carrying a bundle under her left arm and guiding her cane with the right is Mina. She takes slow, deliberate steps. I stare at her. The cooks make sure they save her some of every meal that they prepare. Most days, she makes this trip morning and night. When she is too tired or ill, children are pressed into service to bring her meals. Everyone in the quarters knows that Mina receives this special treatment, and no one complains. She is old.

As Mina passes my doorstep, her sightless eyes see nothing, but her powerful inner senses know I am here. It makes her smile. I feel my usual sense of confusion and dislike for that smile.

"Good mornin', Cousin Pearl, habbin' a good day?" she asks in what I always interpret as a sinister way.

She knows there is no one in the quarters who is having a good day. "Good morning, Auntie Mina. I wish I could say I am, but as you know the sick house and cabins are filled with folks suffering from the strange fever. I am feeling quite helpless at the moment, thank you. There are women losing babies and miscarrying from the fevers. Children are gravely ill. Even the strong men succumb."

"Don' worry, dear girl," she says, still smiling. "You figger it out, you a smart one." With that she steps along.

I feel as if I could strike her in the back. *'Don't worry, girl?'* How dare she? I know that Mina has an idea of what is happening in the quarters that brought on the horrible accidents and now the killing fevers. I think about confronting her. *What do you know about this? Does this all have to do with Ruby?* I swallow the words but the thoughts settle in my mind.

I take another deep breath of the fresh morning air and step back inside the smothering damp heat of the sick house. There is hardly space to move about, crowded with twenty-two mats on the floor. Moans and groans fill the room.

"Please don', please don'," screams Bessie in a delirious state.

"Jesus, Jesus, help me," pleads Alice. I go to calm Bessie, Lizzie attends to Alice. Lizzie's face is drawn, echoing her fatigue. Her shift hangs on her skinny frame.

"Lizzie, go over to Granny's, get something to eat and try to take a nap. I will take care of things here."

"Oh, Cousin Pearl, thank you," she says folding her hands in a prayerful posture.

Just as Lizzie is about to step out the back door, Sally's daughter bursts into the sick house, screaming and crying.

"Mama sick, mama sick, she bleedin'. Please see 'bout mama, Cousin Pearl." Lizzie and I pass a knowing look to each other, she smiles and steps back in.

"I'm sorry, Lizzie."

"Never mind, Cousin Pearl. Dese is hard times."

I grab my bag and race down the path to Sally's cabin. Her four young children, who have become her caretakers, stand around her bed. Her husband, like all the men and women who are not bedridden, is working twice as hard to make up for the loss of hands in the fields. He is not allowed to leave the fields and be here to help his wife.

"Cousin Pearl, mama so sick, she talkin' outta her head. She burnin' up wit feber 'n...." Before she can finish, I see the puddle of blood in which Sallie is lying. She has miscarried.

I say to the oldest children, "Quick, fetch water and cloths for me. If you can't find cloths, get to my cabin and ask Lizzie."

To the youngest I say, "Go to Auntie Ama's. Tell her Cousin Pearl sent you to see if there is any food left." They return empty handed. I then send them to Mina to ask for a few morsels for the children. Meanwhile, I examine Sally, wash her, and stay with her until the men return from the fields in the evening.

"Sorry, Sallie lost the baby," I say baldly as her husband inches near the bed.

Exhausted from doing the work of two men, he can only say, "Thank you for stayin' wid her 'n de chillen."

The fevers have taken a toll on the quarters and on the plantation. For three weeks, the raging sickness affects every cabin. Men and women weak and barely recovered are forced into the fields. Though no one has died but babies and fetuses, the weakest can't seem to recover. Eight women have miscarried during the fevers. Two had stillborn births.

The loss of the babies angers Master Bellamy, and I know I will be blamed. There is a subtle distrust that rests between a midwife and a Master. While Masters need midwives to bring children into the world and keep his hands healthy, all in order to make him rich, they are always suspicious of "African tricks" that midwives will use to deny what they believe is rightfully theirs. When slave women miscarry or when infants die, they become angry at limits to their power.

Tonight as I lie in bed I ask my Abena to come to me and give me advice. *Abena, you saved the lives of so many in the quarters. You knew exactly which herb to use, what tea to give. I know that soon Master Bellamy will punish me for the loss of the babies. I beg you to please come to me and show me what to do.*

Abena does not come to me. Instead I take the path to Mina's cabin.

Mina

I brace myself for the encounter. She is just an old blind woman, I tell myself, but in the next breath, a less confident me says, *But she has a power that no one in the quarters defies.* Ill at ease, I know I must summon the courage to face her because I need help. I step lightly up to her porch.

Hanging above the door is a tuft of raffia. I lift my hand to knock, and as if knowing I was coming this minute, she opens the door. It startles me. I stand on her threshold and am mesmerized by the old woman. She is much smaller in stature than she seems to us. Her petite, brittle, chocolate body is clothed in the consistent black dress covered by the white apron. Her head is covered with the red kerchief she is never without; the women believe she is bald.

"Come in, Cousin Pearl. You have come to the right place for hep. Dat's why dat herb is ober de door, it tell people dey can come here for hep." She adds confidently, "And you have finally come." Her strong voice emanates power, and I feel small, childlike in her presence.

My jaw tightens and I take a deep breath to steady myself. My eyes catch something on the floor in front of the door. It is a face, carved and painted, with two cowrie shells for eyes, one for a nose, one for a mouth. My discomfort develops into fear. *Who is this woman?* I wonder. *Will she hurt me?* I remember Abena saying, "I have become a Christian, and I promised Miss Emily, Master William's wife, that I would not practice any of the African superstition."

I cast my gaze swiftly from one corner of the cabin to the next. There are gourds hanging by hooks, some covered in cloth and feathers. I figure that Mina's concoctions are collected in them. On one side of the room sits a large metal pot with pieces of spikes, knives, nails, a horseshoe and other assorted shapes of iron scattered around it. On the other side are covered clay pots and dishes on the floor, along with bottles decorated with cloth. There is a candle burning in front of these. She has piles of herbs on the floor. There are animal skins hanging from the ceiling in one part of the room: snakes, frogs, lizards, deer, and goat. There are feathers from different birds, and a small pile of animal bones.

My nostrils are invaded by a mixture of plants, perfume, musty dampness, and dried animal skins. I put my hand over my nose to shield my senses. I feel almost intoxicated. There is some strange elegance in this sensory cacophony, a quiet order that seems to connect all of these elements. This cabin, though inhabited only by Mina, contains more life inside its walls than in all of the quarters. On the mantle rests the dried bouquet of lavender tied in a red ribbon made by Ruby and given to each woman before her suicide. In an instant, I know that Ruby's spirit resides here and that I have come to the right place for answers to help heal us.

I leap back when I see the live owl that stares at me from the mantle. Mina laughs.

"You full yet?" she inquires.

It takes a moment for me to understand her meaning before I reply. "Almost. Not quite. Sometime you will have to explain to me what all of this means."

"Means you startin' to understand?"

"Understand what?" I question.

"That Ruby's spirit require us wimmin, and you 'specially, to return to de ol' ways to hep her go home in peace."

"And the old ways?"

"You gots to come home chile, gots to use de Afrique ways to hep you in dese troublin'times.

Ain't gon be no peace in dis here quarters 'til Ruby satisfy. Why you think she hang herself? Ruby a special chile come here 'gainst her own wishes. But you, Cousin Pearl, you couldn't let her li'l spirit be, you has to sabe ebby slave chile you kin to make old Massa rich."

Anger begins to rise up in me; I can feel my face turn warm and red. "I only did what a midwife does, what I am supposed to do. I was born to bring life into this world, save all the little ones I can."

"But dis chile don' want you to sabe 'er. 'Member I was dere? Saw you fightin' wid her, make her be born whedder dat what she want or not. Ruby not like us, you seen it early, too. Dat's why you tries to make her yor own."

"I loved Ruby," I cry. "She was like my own daughter, the child I never had. I understood her, knew she could never be a slave, her spirit wouldn't allow it, but I helped her all I could."

"Didn't love her 'nough. Dat chile come to you firs, say she cain't have no slave baby. You turn her away, say her baby be differnt cuz Sam de daddy, got Bellamy blood, git to work in de Big House. Still a slave. Ain't Sam a slave? Ain't no life for a poor African les' dey lib in de old way, don't never gib de white man de soul. Ruby ain't nebber give hers."

Most of this is nonsense to me. "Why did she kill herself? Why couldn't she trust me to do what was right for her?"

"Ruby sakkerfice herself like yor Jesus did, to save de spirits of de unborn from suffrin' in dis awful place. Dem spirits be torment like Ruby. She cain't bear to know 'nudder spirit suffer like her. She gots to do sumting to make de wimmin see dat bringin' poor little spirits in dis world to be sol' like cattle be wrong. Most, she need *you* to see dat; you must use de Afrique ways to protect de spirits of de unborn babies. Her dyin' meant to gib you and de wimmin in de quarters a message. Ony spirit wants to come and stay here be born to a man and a 'oman dat freely loves each udder. Spirit jus' made to come here for make Bellamy rich cain't be tolerate. Won't be no peace in de quarters 'til we obey. De ancestors angry. Ruby always close to de ancestors, she see and feel tings udders don't. Dat spirit in her stomach angry, don't want to come here."

I drop onto the floor and weep. I didn't know her at all. I look up at the tiny woman. "Do you blame me for all the children born into slavery on this plantation? I am a midwife, God gave me the gift to bring life into the world. What am I to do?"

221

"Abena taught you to forget de old ways so she kin protec' you. It time fo you to come back, chile."

"Abena protected me from what?"

"Chile, dat is for anudda day. You come to see me today, dis is fo what Ruby want. You will soon see ebby ting gon be alright in de quarters."

Sam

Sam has not been himself since Ruby died. He continues to drink heavily every day. He has become more hateful. The field hands complain that he shouts insults and issues lashings more than ever before. The quarters, however, take their liberties every night after Sam passes out from drink. They joke among themselves: "You owns de day, we owns de night." This goes on for weeks but comes to an abrupt end when Percy awakes one night. Instinctively he goes to check the cabins, and then he rings the bell and sounds the alarm. "Niggas havin' their way, cabins empty but for children." He rushes to alert the passed-out Sam. After a good lashing, Sam is now being watched as much as the other slaves.

Sam appears at my door tonight. I can scarcely recognize him, for he is only a ghost of his former self. His once enticing green eyes now sit in blood-red sockets, his almond skin is seamed with dirt, and his ragged, stained clothes hang on his scarecrow body. Most repulsive is the stench of liquor that follows him like a swarm of flies.

"Pearl, I'm sick," he says as he stumbles into the cabin.

"My God, Sam, what has happened to you? I hardly recognize you. What have you done to yourself?" I ask, and then scolding, "What has the liquor done to you?"

"Pearl, it's not the liquor. I am really sick; I drink to numb the pain."

I guide Sam to a vacant pallet and help him lie down as the other sick roll their eyes and nod to each other.

"Where is the pain?" I ask.

Sam points to the middle of his forehead. "A hot beam of fire. No matter what I do, it won't go 'way. Pearl, it's terrible, I can't sleep, don't have any strength to fix a meal, too weak to walk to the kitchen house to get a plate. Doubt they'd give me a plate anyway, rather feed it to the dogs. If they give me food it would probably have poison in it." Some of the sick snicker under covered heads.

I start to remove Sam's filthy shirt. "Let's take this off and let me get a pan of water and wash you, then get you something clean to wear." I put cloths soaked in vinegar on Sam's forehead and fix a tea of sassafras for him while I prepare the bath water. I gently wash Sam's face, neck, and chest.

Suddenly, Sam grabs my hand and tears flow from his eyes. "Pearl, it isn't my fault. I had to hide Ruby's grave or Master Ben would have killed me. I never saw him so angry, almost frothing at the mouth like a mad animal. Said she didn't deserve burial in the slave cemetery, so I had to take her far away and not mark her grave."

"Where is she, Sam? Bad things are happening in the quarters and everyone is afraid worse things are going to happen if we don't send her away properly."

Sam raises up and looks around at the silent covered heads pretending to be asleep.

"Sorry, Pearl, can't tell," Sam says, looking sicker than when he came in. "One day I'll plant a tree. But Pearl, for now, nobody in the quarters can know where Ruby is buried."

Sam weeps silently and soon passes out. The handsome, arrogant driver, abuser of the quarters' women and workers, is helpless. Now more hated than ever before because of the disappearance of Ruby's body, Sam is totally alone. My disgust for him melts as I look down at his face. *He didn't choose the color of his eyes or his skin,* I think. *Would he have been happier being a common field hand rather than the exalted yellow driver, son of a Master? A slave is a slave.*

Sam wakes a short time later. "I think I can go now, Pearl, so you won't get into trouble." He staggers up to leave, peering red-eyed at the others now fully asleep. I give him a cup of horseradish root poultice to put on his forehead.

"Take this and rub it in. It will help."

"Thanks, Pearl."

After this, I make it a habit to observe him instead of ignoring him. I watch him for nights now. Some nights after Percy makes his rounds, Sam leaves his cabin. Tonight I will follow him.

It is a clear night with a full moon lighting the slave street. I wait and out of his cabin comes Sam dragging a large sack. As he passes, I do not get the foul smell of his liquored life that usually floats around and leaves a trail behind him. I let him get a ways ahead, and I follow in and out behind cabins. He stops abruptly, looks behind him, and goes on again. My heart races, praying he will not see me. He goes into the woods. I keep my distance and mark my trail by unwinding a ball of yarn. Sam stops again and sits on the ground, his head between his legs. From my distance, I can hear him weeping and mumbling. I creep a bit closer, hiding behind a bush to hear what he is saying. Just as I find a perfect spot to spy upon him, he grabs his bags and races away, farther into the woods.

I am surprised by the turn he takes. He heads toward the lavender fields, Ruby's favorite place, beelines for a clearing where there is a small pine tree. I stoop low as I make my way through the perfume of the flowers. Sam falls on his knees beside what I now assume is Ruby's grave. He begins to weep again, taking items from his bag – a glass, Ruby's comb and brush, ribbons she wore in her hair, an old bonnet. He holds a locket on a chain through his fingers. I wonder where he got it.

"My sweet Ruby, I love you, and I cannot live without you. You never understood my love for you. I loved you when you were just a girl, I watched you grow and knew I would ask Master Ben to have you as my wife." He wipes his eyes and running nose. There is no smell of stale liquor, the scent of lavender is strong.

He sits back on his haunches. "I am not the animal you think. I, like you, long for freedom, for love. Some time ago I stopped hoping, seeing freedom as impossible. That's when I lost my soul and just became a black body. Ruby, please forgive me for the sins, for every stripe I gave my fellow man and woman. Please forgive me for every woman I forced myself on, for every slave child my seed made. I am like everybody in the quarters. I am a slave. But my burden is worse. Master's blood runs in my veins, and my light skin and green eyes set me apart. Even though he taught me to read, it doesn't help me. I am trusted not by him, not by the quarters."

Sam lowers his head and speaks through his tears. "If you find me to be inhuman, know that I too have no control over my life. I must lash or be lashed, guard the fields or work the fields, produce children or have my manhood sliced away. I know eight children I have fathered; all of the women have husbands. Master Ben and his friends watch as I violate women. The women and their husbands cry. When I'm done, I return to my cabin and shed my tears and drown my conscience with liquor."

I sit like a stone, stunned to hollow silence listening to Sam's story.

"Ruby, years ago a woman I loved was forced to mate with men from other plantations. I begged Ben to buy her but old Colonel Long would not sell. I turned my hatred of Colonel Long and my anger at my situation onto the poor black bodies under my control. Every time I look at those sweaty black, obedient bodies, I hate them as much as I hate myself for not being able to stand up to the white man.

"I knew you were different. I wanted you to have the best life you could have on the plantation. Our child would have Bellamy blood and we would never be separated or sold. He would get a job in the Big House or the diary, like you, no hard work in the fields. But you preferred that farm hand, a cotton picker. You would not allow yourself to even try to love me." His voice grows angry. "Yes, I had Cato sold, but I saved you from being sold. You never knew what I did for you by marrying you. If not for me, you would have been sold South to who knows what fate for plotting to run away with Cato. All I asked was that you try to learn to love me."

Cheeks wet and hands balled into fists, he continues. "Did you really hate me so much, so much, Ruby, that you would kill yourself and our child? Why, Ruby, why? That child that I wanted with all of my heart was an indication that this poor black body has been on this earth. Ruby, family is all that lets us slaves know that we are human. And all I ever wanted is a family. I wanted a family with you." Tears gush from Sam's eyes and he lets them rain on his chest.

"I know I am the most hated man in the quarters, but what am I to do?" He stops talking for a minute, sobbing uncontrollably. He finally runs out of tears. "You said you hated me since the day I beat Roy. Why couldn't you understand? I have to do what I'm told or I'm sold. I am a cursed man, too black to run away and be a white man, and too white to be trusted in the quarters. Ruby, I am torn and weary. I can't live without the promise of what could have been, so I join you and hope that in that world, wherever it may be, we will make our peace."

Sam leans over with the locket in his hand, kisses it and places it on the grave. He looks around at the lavender field and I freeze with my eyes closed, praying he will not see me. It is quiet, and I open my eyes to see him pulling a handful of lavender flowers. He arranges them on the grave, and gets up and walks purposefully toward the woods. I crawl on my knees through the field, trying not to be spied by him. I follow him down to the creek that runs alongside the heavy timber. He stumbles, and without hesitation suddenly throws himself into the creek. My hand flies to my mouth and I want to call out to him, to stop him, but my words cannot escape. He falls face down in the water and does not struggle. He is carried along by the current.

I am numb. I fall to my knees. Salty tears flow down my cheeks. I have just seen Sam take his life and done nothing. Ruby had come to me only days before her suicide and I had done nothing. I, the midwife, the one who brings life into the world, have stood by helpless as Ruby and now Sam found their freedom through death. I walk back to Ruby's grave, now clearly marked by her belongings that Sam brought.

I must tell Mina and the quarters that I have found Ruby's grave. But how do I tell that I was there when Sam drowned and I did nothing? I take a deep breath and wish that when I wake his drowning will only be a nightmare dream.

Where Is Sam?

I am awakened this morning when Percy bursts open Sam's door, ready to lash the inebriated driver. The horrible night rushes back into my mind. I jump up and watch Percy through my window. I know there is no Sam. Percy calls the workers to the front of Sam's cabin and inquires of everyone.

"Have you seen that lazy no good Sam?"

"No, Massa."

"Surely he did not try to run; he's too much of a drunkard for that."

After working in the fields all day the men return as usual. I have not told anyone about Sam or that I know the whereabouts of Ruby's grave now. I have a headache like an axe is stuck in my temple and have told the women and Lizzie that I need rest. The men are ordered out to search the woods for Sam. Within a short while, they return with his body, carrying it awkwardly down the slave street. The whole quarters, curious about the fate of the hated driver, come out of their cabins to follow the procession.

"What happen to ol' Sam?"

"Look like he drown, find him tangle up in some tree limb at the side a de creek."

"He fall or he pushed?"

"Musta been drunk and falled in." There is much laughter from the crowd, and I am ashamed that I cannot stand up for him, tell them he was sober as a stone. My headache pounds and I am cringing in my heart. I do not go out of my cabin.

"Y'all tink it was Ruby done dribe him crazy?"

"Don't know. All I know, couldn't stop drinking dat liquor. Drank hisself to death."

Percy, scowling, growls, "Well, get him in the ground. Y'all dig a hole and git dis nigga ready to bury," he orders. "Someone will pay for this."

"Got to prepare him first," the men say. Even Sam the hated driver deserves a decent burial, if not for respect, out of fear. The quarters can't have Sam's spirit hanging around. Without a proper burial, Sam's spirit cannot go to its final destination and will like Ruby wreak havoc.

I can tell by the non-committal looks on the faces of the women that none are interested in touching Sam's body.

I go to my door. "Bring Sam to the sick house," I say numbly.

"I will help you, Cousin Pearl," volunteers Bina.

As the men lay Sam on the pallet, I look into his now grotesquely bloated face. My tears flow. *Is there something I could have done to prevent your death, Sam?* I ignore Bina's questioning look at the tears I can't stop. We wash Sam and wrap him in a sheet. The men then carry him to the slave cemetery followed by all of us in the quarters.

"Sure don't want his spirit 'roun here."

"Let's git him in the groun' quick."

The quarters return after a swift burial. Rather than somber, they are spirited. Bina, Sallie, and Fannie stop in the sick house to share their feelings.

"Hate to speak ill of de dead, but dat Sam was a rascal. He hab me in fron' a my lovin' husband John," spits out Fannie.

"I glad Ruby come back fer 'im. Hate de way he made dat poor chile marry him."

"Dat one man de quarters won't miss."

"Tink cause he got dat white blood in 'im, he bedder dan de res' of us," Sally says, unthinking for a moment of my blood, the same as Sam's.

Her hand goes to her mouth, she bows her head and speaking in an embarrassing whisper apologizes. "I sorry, Pearl, you ain't nuthin like Sam."

"You don't have to apologize. I understand," I say putting a good face on the shame that I feel. Tonight, I want to be more like them, dark brown, African looks and ways. *Do you speak ill of me when you women are gathered?* I shake off the thought.

"'Nough excitement for one day," says Bina, motioning to the others to leave.

"Good night, get some rest, it's late already," I say.

Still I have not told them about Ruby's grave. I despise my cowardice.

Bellamy blood means that I don't have to labor in the fields, that I can do the work I love. But as Ruby often reminded me, I too was enslaved, and worse yet, I did Bellamy's bidding and increased his wealth by ensuring that he had healthy workers and a steady supply of slave babies. But what would the quarters do without me? I cannot let them suffer even if they must return to the fields. Do I believe that I am different and better than the women who labor in the fields? Did Abena feel that way? Why did she discourage me from anything African? How can I become more like them? How I can I find the African part of me? I am lost.

The Lash

I watch as the field hands return from work. Saturday afternoon, time off from the fields but still plenty of chores to be done. After a brief respite, the slaves have to scrub their cabins. Percy demands clean cabins, on orders from Miss Charlotte, and they both inspect unannounced. Gardens must be tended and chickens taken care of. Clothes have to be scrubbed in the big black pot. The men must go fishing and hunting to provide extra meat for families for the Saturday night meal because by Saturday afternoon, there is nothing left in the cabins to eat. Rations are not passed out until after church on Sunday morning.

I am surprised to hear Percy ringing the bell calling all of the quarters to the open field where slaves are scolded, given orders, and stripes. A feeling of dread runs through me like a chill as I wonder which poor soul will be the victim of Percy's wrath today.

My thoughts are interrupted by the violent entrance of Master Ben and Percy into the sick house. I gasp as my heart races.

"Master Ben, Percy, what is it? Is someone deathly ill?" I ask. Master Ben's reddened face is twisted into a scowl, Percy smiles sinisterly. I peer at the whip in Master Ben's hand and my confusion instantly turns into fear. I stand trapped in this uneasy space, too afraid to cry, waiting for what seems an eternity for Master Ben to speak.

"Wench, you get your ass out here," he says so close to my face that I smell his foul liquored breath.

"You betrayed me, you tried to ruin me by killing all those babies with what you call fever. I knew that no matter what my mother said, I couldn't trust you. You are just like every other nigga on this plantation. Bellamy blood or not. Can't trust any of you." He glares at me. "And I think it was your influence that had something to do with making that girl hang herself."

I gasp.

"And now probably because of you one of my best breeder men is drowned."

The tears gush from my eyes as I try to speak. I know I cannot speak of Ruby. I stammer, "M…Master Ben, I didn't do anything. It was the fever, even Dr. Smith…."

Master Ben cuts me off.

"Shut your lying mouth. You are right, you did nothing; that is, nothing to save the babies. Ten babies are dead. Half the quarters is too sick to work. Do you know how much you cost me?"

"But Master, I...." He pushes me through the door, grabs my hair and uses it to drag me to the whipping field. I stumble behind him and I see everyone in the quarters staring in disbelief. I am the midwife; after Sam, the most powerful slave in the quarters. I have Bellamy blood and nothing ever happens to me. I go to Master Ben on their behalf, and now here I am about to be lashed in front of them. I avert my eyes in shame as tears flow down my cheeks. Percy rips off my blouse and forces me to the ground. He ties my hands and feet to stakes. There is total silence. I can feel the anticipation and smell the fear of the quarters, as well as my own. I wait and then it comes. The first stripe is like fire ripping open the skin of my back, I scream out in pain and hear some of the women scream. Children begin to bawl.

Percy yells, "Shut up that damn noise or you will be next. Master is giving this wench what she deserves." I cannot believe that Ben is hurting me in this way. I am, after all, his sister – same father. I try to move my hands and feet as I feel Ben rearing back to give the next stripe.

"Please, Master Ben, please have mercy," I scream as I try to raise my head. The next strip is more brutal than the first, and each that follows tears more deeply into my back. My whole body is afire.

My face is submerged in a pool of muddy tears wept as I am lashed. I drift in and out of consciousness as fifty stripes are laid on my naked back. Master Ben, finally exhausted, throws the whip to the ground and walks away. The front of his pants is wet as though he has relieved himself. Only after he and Percy are safely away does the crowd rush to me. I hear them talking, they are circling around me like bees, each woman doing something to soothe my pain.

"Hep me git her up!" yells Bina, as she unties the ropes that hold my arms. I feel Bina trying to raise my head from the ground but lacking the strength to do so. Luther, Bina's husband, unties my feet. Luther and Lacy, his brother, gently lift my viciously beaten body and follow Bina and the other women into my cabin. Every step they take, as gently as they try to carry me, is torture. I am consumed by the fire of pain.

"Lay her here," insists Bina as she points to a quilt quickly placed on the floor. She has assumed charge of my care, and the men ease me face down. She dips cool water from the gourd and gently turns my head and wipes my face. I try to lift my head and speak.

"Sush, easy now," says Bina as she strokes my hair.

"It gonna be alright, Pearl. We gonna take good care of you," she says reassuringly. By now it seems that every woman in the quarters has crowded into my cabin. I can feel the heat of their bodies surrounding me and their calloused fingers gently trying to remove my clothing. I hear their muffled sobbing.

"What you need, Bina?" asks Daisy.

"Look in Pearl's jars, get some salve quick."

"Susie, you and Hannah help me ease her skirt off. Just gon cover her lightly with this cloth."

I try to open my eyes but can see only blurs. I want to say something, to thank them, but my tongue is in the way. Tears stream down my face.

"Dat bastard flay her real bad," curses Bina, speaking to no one in particular. "Dis gon hurt a bit, Pearl, but it got to be done."

I scream and faint as the salve is applied to my raw back.

When I come to they're still talking. "I knows, darlin', but I got to do dis," says Bina in a soft voice. She is no longer touching me. "I know it pain you, it be ober now.

"Bring cool water. Lift her head gentle now, just a sip at a time," she orders. Several of the women – Daisy, Susie, and Bertha – sit on the floor near me and begin to soothe me with handmade fans. They chant, "We love you, Cousin Pearl, we love you."

I weep for their kindness.

In all my days, 1 have never experienced physical misery. Having never had a child of my own, I witnessed but never knew the pain of all those women screaming out in childbirth. I have wept and cared for the men and women who were lashed, but this is my misery, a new and surprising horror that I have never known personally, that one cannot imagine even having seen it.

Hannah kneels close to my face and gently opens my mouth and spoons in bitter tea little by little.

"Dis will make you sleep, baby. Soon won't feel no pain, jus sleep." The waves of pain and fire are so great that I try to reach for the cup so that I can just sleep away. I attempt to lift up to get more, but Hannah shakes her head. "No, baby, dis enouf."

The women cover my exposed buttocks and legs with a clean cloth. Bina leans in and whispers "Sleep now, baby. We gon take care of you this time."

Bina calls the women to sit in a circle around me on the cabin floor. Before I drift off, I hear snatches of their plans for me.

"We got to figure out a way to care for Pearl. She done took care a us all dis time, habben a chile or sick. Now it our time to take care a her."

"How we gon do dat?" asks Susie. "We workin' all day."

"Massa real mad at Pearl, say he don care if she die. Ain't nebber seen Massa beat no slave hisself. He shore mad at Pearl."

"Well, mad or not, Pearl need some takin' care of," insists Bina. "What we gon hab to do is make a plan. We gon hab to take turn bein sick for a while. Susie, you done had de fever. Got to git real sick in the field tomorrow, take a little dose of bloodroot to help you vomit your breakfast. Pass right out, den me and Daisy help you back. Slip ober here to Pearl and see 'bout her. You gon hab to be sick fo a while. When all de udders off to de field

243

you come ober here and see after Pearl. And one more ting — tell Mina we need her help," instructs Bina.

"When we comes in from the field, some gots to come on in here see 'bout Pearl while de udders make de food for all de families. We got to really be one now. Ain't no Bina, no Sally, no Susie, no Daisy, just one, we all jus one."

The women, some with tears streaming down their faces, embrace and begin to plan for the weeks ahead, the time that it will take me to recover from the lashing.

The women, all but Bina, leave the cabin. She makes a pallet on the floor next to me and gently strokes my hair and face each time I moan.

"Don't worry, Pearl, Massa tink he done kill de queen bee, but he jus stir up de nes' fo sho." Bina drifts off to sleep, but not before asking Ruby for advice. "Ruby, I know how you hate dis old slavery, nouf to kill yor ownself. Dey say you jus like yor Ibo pa, say no Ibo cain't be no slave for long, kill dey self. We need you, Ruby. You dun drove ol Sam crazy, so we know you still here. Now tell us how to make Massa pay for what he done to Pearl."

Book III
1861–1865

Awakening

I am coming out of a dreamlike state. I feel as though I am in a different world. All of my senses are attuned to sights unseen, scents unsmelled, and unfamiliar sounds. I have the distinct sensation that I am floating, perhaps enclosed in a womb like that of the babies that I birth. I am surrounded by warmth, the pungent smell of herbs bubbling on the boil. Chants in a tongue unknown to me bombard my ears. I lift my head to see Mina's cloudy blue-gray unseeing eyes roll back into the top of her eyelids as she chants "Yemaya Assessu, Assessu Yemaya, Yemaya Olodo, Olodo Yemaya."

My eyes focus on items I have seen in Mina's cabin. Her clay pots sit on mats inside my room. Stretching my neck as far as possible, I see one of the black cauldrons from Mina's cabin with something steaming out of it. Pots and dishes line the hearth. Smoked fish and opossum, toasted corn, fruit, peppers are piled on dishes. Bottles filled with unknown liquids sit nearby. A gourd covered with bird feathers hangs in a corner. On the table are bunches of herbs, along with bowls of ashes and white chalk. The entire room -- the walls, the ceiling, the window, the door-- is covered in black cloth. *Is all of this a dream?*

Mina approaches my bed, in one hand a black cock feather and salve, a bowl of mush in the other. She sits next to me on my bed, gently touches my face.

"Daughter, it time fo you to wake now. Time fo yor real healin' to begin. Dis de bes' ointment fo you, mix togedder scrofula, china berry root, and bluestone, boil it all down and mix it wid dis pure hog lard. Now let me put dis on yor back." The odor of the salve, though not offensive, overpowers my nostrils even as it soothes my scarred back. When Mina finishes with the salve, she covers my back with a white cloth.

"I tink it time fo you to sit up now, gits your strength back; been on yor belly a long time." Mina pulls her chair close to my bed and lifts me as I painfully sit up.

"Easy, you in Mina's hans now. You be jus' fine. Open yor mouf, chile, got to gits some corn meal mush in you." She pushes a large spoonful into my mouth and dips her spoon for more.

Mina feeds me like an infant, spoons mush in, wipes my mouth. I am grateful, confused and ashamed because the old woman I have feared and resented so long is now my caretaker.

After I finish the mush, Mina says, "Daughter, now we mus' talk." My eyes open wide, and my heart starts to pound. This is going to be a conversation that will change my life in some way.

Abena

Mina takes Granny Abena's delivery bag from the hook on which it hangs near the fireplace and brings it to me. I hold it to my chest, a pang of sadness rushing over me. *I wish you were here. Granny, I miss you and I need you.*

"Now chile," says Mina. "You tell me yor story of Abena, and I will tell you mine. When dey bof put togedder, yor spirit be free."

Though I do not quite understand what Mina's words mean, I begin to tell the story that Abena told me of her capture, voyage to Charleston, and enslavement on the Bellamy plantation. As I talk, I can hear Granny Abena's voice in my head just like when I first heard the story.

"'Mama was sick so she sent me to the neighboring village to administer to a woman who was slow to recover from the birth of her baby. Mama was known as one of the best midwives in the area.'" *Abena, you talked to me with such pride in your voice.*

"'I was walking through the forest when what appeared to be a large net was thrown over me. I struggled to free myself but was lifted into the air and struck by one of the men. When I awoke my ankles and wrists were chained and I was lying in a spot where 30 or more individuals were also chained. I could not understand what was happening.'" *I remember tears started to flow down your cheeks, Abena.*

"'I wept constantly as I was forced to walk chained with the other captives. I was made to understand that if I didn't stop crying, I would be beaten like some of the others. I could only think of my parents, especially Mama. She would be so worried. What would she think? Would she feel responsible somehow for sending me to the village?'

"'After we had walked for many days, we came to a large castle and were put into the dungeon for days. We were hungry, tired, stripped naked, and all of the women's jewelry taken. For reasons I've never known I was allowed to keep the little leather herb bag that I wore around my neck. One day we were rowed out to a boat larger than any I had ever seen in my life. *What is happening? Where are we going?* I thought. *This is a mistake, I am Abena. I am a midwife.* 'I am needed in my village,' I screamed. But the strange men with pale skin, red faces, and thin stringy hair did not understand me, nor was I able to understand their strange tongue.'

"'I struggled to avoid getting on the big boat but I was thrown aboard where I found many more people, from different villages and tribes. The men and women were shoved into separate spaces on the boat. The trip lasted many, many moons. Countless women became very ill, others died. Some went insane. I did what I could to comfort them, and when possible, I placed just a pinch of the herbs on their tongue to help them to relax.' " *I can see you, Abena, as you kiss the herb bag.* 'Several women went into labor on the ship. I tried to assist them as much as possible. All of the babies and two of the women died.'"

I recalled Abena then breaking into loud painful sobs. She gathered herself and went on telling me her tale.

"'The captain noticed my assistance to the women around me and began to use me to help with other sick men and women captives. I became hopeful and thought that perhaps if I helped the sick, they would understand that this was a mistake and return me to my village.'

"'The very first night the men of the ship came into the women's area and took three or four young girls. The girls thinking they were going to be killed screamed and fought back as much as they

253

could, but they of course were overpowered by the men. When they returned, bloody and beaten, the women knew that their fate was not death but nearly as bad. I did what I could to comfort the poor girls, many as young as ten. Some drifted into despair, not eating or speaking, others went insane. They thrashed about, shrieked, and dug their nails into their skin until blood was drawn. It was horrible.'"

Oh, Abena. I see her clearly, shaking her head in agony as she continued her story.

"'I kept thinking that the strange men would not take me if I could just show how helpful I could be.'

"'One night the captain of the ship summoned me. I thought that perhaps someone was ill who needed my attention. I was wrong.'" Granny Abena lowered her head as if ashamed. l remembered smoothing her hair and whispering into her ear, *It is over now, Granny, you are here safe with me.*

"'As it turned out, the captain had not only noticed my skills but my beauty. He kept me in his cabin. At 13 years of age, I was raped, many times. By the time we reached Charleston, I was pregnant with his child, your mother.'"

Abena wiped her eyes, composed herself, and continued. "'I had never seen anything like what

254

they called Charleston.'" She had shaken her head and laughed to herself. "My whole body was trembling; I stood there in disbelief biting my lips. The sun was beating down, and there were people everywhere, yelling, talking in strange tongues. I started to feel sick from the smell of palm oil, pipe smoke, and sour water in puddles. Even in the marketplace in my village with all of the women chattering and bartering, there was never this much noise. The captain pushed me along through the crowded streets.'

"'We came to a large enclosure with high walls guarded by men.'" *Remember, Abena, that you showed me how you looked up and gauged the height of the walls with your hands?* "'Here we were fed better than we had eaten aboard the ship. We got to wash, and they gave us clean clothes. The captain assured me that my lot would be better than the rest because of my craft. I would not have to stand naked on the auction block but would be sold directly to his friend, Colonel William Bellamy, who owned a cotton plantation on an island near Charleston. I wondered, though. How could my lot be better than the rest? I am chained, I am spoiled by this strange white man, and I am far from my village.'

"'In a few days, this Bellamy came. I was called into a room.'

"'This is the one I sent word to you about,' said the Captain. 'Abena will make a fine nurse and midwife. Already has skills and has a good disposition.'

"Bellamy looked me over while Captain stood back and smiled, proud of his find. Bellamy studied my arms, my teeth, and he had me turn around; he spared me the indignity of taking off my dress. I was sold to Bellamy for $850.'

"A mixture of conflicting feelings streamed through me, hatred for the white man who had defiled my body and was selling me like a bag of grain, but gratitude when we passed a screen where I saw ten or more men pulling the breasts and touching the private parts of the captured women. *What kind of people are these,* I wondered. *What horrible acts await me when I reach the plantation of this Colonel Bellamy? He is to be my master I have been told.*

"'What happened is that I became the midwife and nurse on this plantation. The mistress, Miss Emily, was pleased when I delivered my baby Malaika myself. In my language, her name means angelic beautiful girl, and she *was* the most beautiful girl. When I held her next to my heart I loved her despite the circumstances by which she came to be. I touched her tiny hands and toes and my heart was filled with joy. I not only nursed my own child but also the other babies of the women who worked all day in the fields. I was sad and lonely, wanting my family back home, but when I saw the lives of the women who were beaten, raped, and forced to work in the fields from sun-up to sundown, I began to believe that the Captain was right -- my lot was better. He told me that I could have a life different from the rest if I practiced my craft by keeping the field hands healthy enough to work and made sure that plenty of healthy slave babies were born. And loving the babies helped me. I decided to do whatever was necessary to survive.'

"Granny Abena's last words to me before she died were these: 'I survived to protect you, to teach you how to live as best you can in this life. This is all there is, make the best of it until you reach the other side.'"

I closed Abena's bag and gave it back to Mina and wiped the tears from my eyes. I hoped that Granny Abena would visit me in my dreams.

The Promise

Mina and I sat in chairs facing each other. Mina positioned herself so that her unseeing eyes directly faced mine. She began telling her story about my grandmother Abena.

"Dere was a time when yor Granny Abena and me was friends. But den tings happen and she go her way and do her medicine and me anudder way to do mine. I stuck to de old Afrique ways. Tings happen dat made Abena change."

l looked questioningly into Mina's eyes.

"Was a time when Abena would hep dem slave girls wid de herbs jus' like me. When dey rape by de white man, dey go and Abena gib dem sumting so dey don't hab no baby. She do dat up til de time yor mama died."

"What do you mean?" I ask.

"Let me go way back, chile."

"Yor mama de prettiest chile I ever did see. So pretty she look like a doll. Don't even look real she so pretty. Miss Emily, Massa William's wife, treat yor mama jus like she treat you. Hab her up at de big house, teach her to read, jus make her a pet. Tink she bedder dan de res of us niggas. But yor mama also

259

weak and sickly. She always sick. She jus as sick as she was pretty.

"Den dat smallpox come. Was ebbywhere. Folks was sick and dyin' ebby which way. It come here to Bellamy as well. Abena use her head, she a smart woman. She go out and find de herbs and make a tea dat start to heal all dem workers. Got dem well. Chile, dat was a time. Sick house was always fill up. And dey was so sick. She heal dem all by herself, workin' day and night to heal dem slaves. Den dat Miss Emily come to Abena cryin' and beggin' her to save her son."

The old woman twisted her lips. "I tell you is coz it real important. Let's go back to yor mama, Malaika. Well, dat girl caught the smallpox, too. Tot she was gonna die. Abena stay by her side all de time, jus bathin' her and gib her dat special tea she make. It take a long time but yor mama finally start to git better.

"Abena at de sick house treatin' folks and yor mama was tol' to stay in bed. Sumting got into dat girl dat day and her feber min' tell her to go up to de arbor. Now, we niggas don't suppose to be up dere unless we tol' too. Yor mama gots caught up dere by dat Felix, Miss Emily's boy. Well, he rape dat pore sick girl. She made it back to de cabin but she nebber

260

tol ' Abena 'bout de rape. Yor mama startin' gittin' sick all de time, couldn't keep nuthin' on her stomik. Chile jus' sick. Finally, Abena figure out she wid chile. Yor mama scare to tell but Abena get the story. Dat's where I comes in. Abena come to me to see what we can do for de chile, but it too late, got to have de baby."

"Granny never told me this, "I say in astonishment.

"Yor mama had de baby, dis was you, Pearl. All of us dere to help Abena try to save her but de girl too sick to hab a baby. She die when you born. Abena was mad and sad. I nebber seed her like dat before. She hate dat old Felix.

"Den dat low-down Felix caught de smallpox, the doctor couldn't do nuthin' for him. Old Miss Emily come to Abena cryin' 'n beggin' her to save her son.

"Abena tol Miss Emily'bout de rape. De woman cry 'n cry cause she know Abena hab the way to kill or heal old Felix. Miss Emily beg and beg. Finally, Abena say she heal him but she need sumting in return.

"Dat where you come in."

"What did Granny Abena want in return?"I ask anxiously.

"Abena say she heal Felix if Miss Emily promise dat no white man put his hans on you. Dat you nebber be sold, and dat you be train by her to be de midwife at Bellamy. But mos' important, you don't be made to have no man you don't want, and dat no Bellamy or dere friends ebber touch you. Now she make Emily swear on de Bible dat you would always be protect."

"It means Master Ben is my half brother and Miss Emily is my grandmother. Why Sam always called me cousin, because we are the same blood."

"Yes, dat why you treated different from de rest of us niggas. Dey likes dem niggas bedder who look like dem. Put dem in de Big House to work, dey don't have to work in de hot sun and rain like de res' of us. Dat why when you little you be all up at de Big House and Miss Emily teach you to read."

"Now I am beginning to understand," I say, though still unclear on many things. "Miss Emily always said she was teaching me to read so I could be a good midwife and nurse, so I could help the doctor when I was needed. I understood this, because of Granny Abena always telling me also. But I didn't know exactly that my Granny made a deal with Mistress Emily that saved me."

"Well, Abena save dat bastard Felix. But she real smart ya know. She cut a little piece a his hair when he sleep and real sick. She gib it to me for safe keepin'. Say might hab to use it someday. I takes it and puts it away."

"Dat old Felix got bedder and he start again to look at dese nigga gals. He catch anudder one and rape her too. Abena care for the poor gal. Hurt real bad, say she won't ebber be able to hab chillen. So Abena come to me and say kill de bastard. He done it again like he done to my sweet baby. I took his hair, mixed it with some graveyard dirt, snake skin, some roots and bound it wid black string. Den I dug a hole, place it inside, bury it for his misdeeds. And sometime later de ol' bastard fall off de horse he ridin, hit his head and die. Me and Abena don't nebber talk about it again."

"After dat, I tink Abena feel guilty. Say she gon be a Christian and ask forgibness. Say she jus gone be a good midwife and bring dem babies into de world. Abena love deliverin' dem babies, say it de gift God give her and she wasn't gon to make God mad again. She tink maybe she los her sweet girl cause she hep dem girls what got pregnant. She jus go to studin' her Bible and bein' a good Christian.

"Abena try to do the way she learned in Afrique in dis here place. But dis place ain't like Afrique. Dem babies born here ain't gone be like in Africa. Dey gon be slaves, don't nebber do what dey true destiny call for. Village can guide and shape 'em for good, here dey jus' be like a horse or cow, not treat like human."

"Ebby ting she do, she do for you, Pearl. She make the Massa happy by keepin' dese niggas healthy and keep dem babies comin'. She always want to know as soon as a gal is wid chile so she can try to make sure it don' die in dem first nine days. She make sure Massa hab plenty a babies to sell jus to protec' you. She always tink dat if she do what de Massa want, dat one day he gib you yor freedom. After yor mama die, she jus do whatebber nessary to protec' you. Ebby ting dat woman do, she do for you. She luv you more dan anyting."

I think about what Granny used to say to me -- *Do whatever you can to survive in this world as a slave. Your life is better than the rest. Just do your job well, keep the field hands healthy so they can work and keep those mothers and babies alive for the master. The master is depending on you to birth healthy slave babies.*

"I was dere when you deliver Ruby," says Mina. "Dat a chile do not wan be born in dis here cruel worl' ob slavery. But you gon make her be born anyway. Dat chile fight you like de debil but you won' let go. Dat Ruby nebber belong here, she allus unhappy bein' a slave. Her spirit nebber happy. I jus shake my head when dat chile born, know right den she diffrent," Mina says.

"And you are right, Mina," I said. "I believe Ruby was angry with me all her life. Blamed me for bringing her in to this world as a slave. But I am a midwife; that is the gift God gave me. Am I not to do God's will?"

Mina answers me. "Is it God's will dat dose poor little babies so precious have to grow up in bondage, nebber having no freedom none of dere life? Why you tink so many of dem babies jus gib up and die when dey can?. In dem nine days, dey ain't really in dis world, deciding if dey want to stay. Dem who don't wants to be no slave goes back."

I ask, "Why didn't Ruby leave in those nine days, God knows she tried."

A wry smile crosses Mina's face. "Maybe once dat chile forced to be born, dat chil had sumting she coud do, sumting special. Maybe one

265

day you will know." I am puzzled by her, but she talks on.

"In de old ways, we know dem Abiku babies. Dey come and die seben times. Dey got strong will and do dangers tings. Danger calls dem. In de village we puts a copper chain on de babies ankle to secure dem to de world so dey will not leave. Pearl, my daughter, you mus' be born again in the Afrique way and learn the ways of yor ancestor midwives. Den you hab real power. When you reborn, you will hab the power to lead de women in de quarters."

The Rebirth

Mina declares, "Now Pearl, it is time for yor journey in de womb to end. Time to be reborn. Dis yor las' day in de womb."

Mina calls Lizzie, who has taken over my sick duties. Lizzie takes the black cloths from the walls and replaces them with white cloths. Mina rips the half shift covering my hips and legs. "When I rips dese old cloths, dat means you gittin' rid a yor old life, you free a Abena's promise to de white folks, you bein' born into a new life in de old ways."

She washes me with herb soap and river water. I can feel the herbs gently scratch my skin. "Dis water like de water in de womb." After the bath, Lizzie hands Mina a dead hen and pigeon. Mina strokes my face, neck, arms, hands, legs, feet, front and back with the hen and pigeon. *What is happening to me?* I wonder.

Shockingly, Mina begins to cut my long thick hair; I jerk away but am pulled back by the strong grip of her hands. I squirm and tears flow down my cheeks as she roughly shaves me bald. Mina then washes my head with water and herbs. It feels very good. I feel lighter. I cease crying.

Two pots are placed in front of us, one for Mina and one for me. My hair is placed in a pot filled with herbs. Mina puts her fingers around the necks of the hen and pigeon and twists their heads off and puts them in my pot. I let out a gasp, unprepared for the flowing blood. She holds the birds over her pot and then my pot until all the blood drains. Then she places the bodies of both birds in front of both of our pots. She pours liquor on top of them, some into her pot, then my pot. She places a drop of honey on the bird heads in my pot and pours honey on top of the bird bodies. Lizzie collects the birds onto one plate and takes them outside where Bina and Sallie pluck, clean, and cook them.

When they're done, Mina brings them and other food and places it, along with the liquor, in front of our pots. The same ritual is done for what she calls my "ancestor pot" with the inclusion of a rooster. I am told that this pot is a vessel through which my ancestors can work to assist me and the other women on the plantation. In front of this pot, in addition to a plate of food and liquor, Mina places cups of water, coffee, sugar water, blue colored water, and tea.

Mina gives me one more herb bath, washes my shaved head once more and dries me with white cotton cloth. I am dressed in white clothes, and my head is trubanned in a white scarf. Mina, Lizzie, and I wait, and all of the women in the quarters come to my cabin. They stand at the entrance and I emerge, reborn. As the women embrace me, I sense a new respect and I do indeed feel a sense of power I had not known before. This evening we enjoy a feast of all of the birds that had been prepared for the tuning of my body to the spiritual energies that will henceforth guide and protect me.

That night, Granny Abena and Ruby come to me in a dream where we sit in the lavender field that Ruby loved. Ruby just smiles and Granny Abena speaks to me. "My darling Pearl, your cabin became the womb and Mina the mother who nurtured you. A woman's womb is the greatest power that she possesses. From it, she has the power to nurture, to grow, and to create new life. A woman's womb not only births children but also holds the power to produce great change in ourselves and others. Use the power of your womb to birth a rebellion of the women in the quarters." Ruby nods her head in agreement and my womb begins to undulate feverishly, as if I am going into labor.

Then I sleep until dawn.

The Womb Rebellion

It is a late moonless night; Percy, the men, and all the children in the quarters are well asleep. Newborn Pearl gives instructions to the women: "Go into the woods; loosen a ball of yarn to guide you back. When you get to the fork in the path, go toward the lavender field. Walk through the field. You will see a small pine tree. Beneath its bows is Ruby's grave. Sam has placed dishes and other articles that belonged to Ruby there."

Lizzie and I wait for what seems like hours for the women to return. When they reach my cabin, they are exhausted and fall to the floor. Lizzie quickly passes a gourd of water. The crowded cabin is warm and filled with the smells of women's sweat and the bitter brew boiling in a big black pot in the fireplace. As I sit up on my bed, the women line the floor in a half-circle in front of me. Leaning in, I listen intently to their story of visiting Ruby's grave.

Bina and Fannie take charge of the gathering of women. They walk quietly down the dark slave street, tapping lightly on doors, gathering each of the women. Sallie and Hannah stop at Mina's cabin to help guide her. Once they are at the edge of the woods, they light their lanterns and take the path I described to them. They are as surprised as I to find the grave almost in clear sight. Once they reach it, they place the lanterns near the mound and form a circle around it and begin to clap their hands and stamp their feet while Mina beats a rhythm on the forest floor with her cane. Fannie begins a chant to which the women respond by walking in a circle around the grave.

"Ruby, sweet Ruby," chants Fannie.

"Ruby, sweet Ruby" repeat the women, all the while shuffling and sliding in the circle.

"I know you here, Ruby," chants Fannie.

"I know you here, Ruby." The women place their hands on their foreheads and stretch their necks as if looking for Ruby.

"Speak to me, Ruby," calls Fannie.

"Speak to me, Ruby," chant the women with hands held behind their ears.

As they hasten their steps, the women hold their dress tails, wiggle their hips, and sway their bodies.

They repeat the chant until they are a frenzy of movement waiting for Ruby.

Finally, Ruby's spirit enters Bessie -- her body stiffens and shakes furiously. Bessie's eyes roll back in her head, she spins round and round, flinging her arms and thrashing about. The sight of blood running down Bessie's legs abruptly stops the dancing, and the women stand in shocked amazement. Unintelligible words blurt from Bessie's mouth, and the voice they recognize is Ruby's.

"No more slave babies, no more slave babies, no more slave babies," the possessed Bessie sings over and over in Ruby's voice. Then the exhausted girl falls to the ground.

Crying women grab each other, hug and kiss. Mina speaks to Ruby. "Rest, Ruby, we hear you. We lead you home." The women gathered around Bessie, wipe the sweat from her brow and clean the blood from her legs. They gather their lanterns. Sallie and Hannah guide Mina back through the lavender field and the woods, the women following.

I know that Ruby's spirit will not rest until there are no more enslaved babies born on Bellamy's plantation. It will be up to me, the reborn midwife, protected now by Yemaya, the African spirit of midwives, to lead the women in a womb rebellion. I also know that Mina, the midwife for my rebirth, will guide me in my new role.

The Plan

I call a meeting of the women of the quarters to make a plan to appease Ruby's restless spirit. We meet at Mina's deep into the night, Mina sitting in her rocking chair in front of the fireplace. Each woman brings three small bottles or gourds. I sit at Mina's feet and participate as her eager student.

The old woman has two gourds filled with herbs sitting at her feet. She picks up the first gourd and bends her head to smell it.

"Dis is de black law root mix wid a lil' bluestone, 'n "dis" -- she smells the mixture in the next gourd -- "is bloodroot tea mix wid red pepper and a pinch a gunpowder. Now, each ones of you wimmins needs to take a lil' of each evvy time de moon change, take a lil' from each bottle and won't be no babies." The women laugh, hug each other and on knees crawl up to Mina to get the mixture.

"Now dat's only half de plan. Pearl gone tell y'all de res'."

"We will fake pregnancies that will end in miscarriage," I say. The women stretch their eyes in amazement.

"So how we gone fake us be with chile?" asks Lillie.

"You jes' wait. Patience," Mina scolds. "Dat Pearl one smart gal,"

I hold out my hand in which is a batch of all lengths of straw.

"What we will do is to pull straws; half of the women, those with the shortest straws, will be with child first. When it's time, I will report to Miss Caroline that you are with child." The women wait, excitement on their faces.

"I will say that your food ration must be increased because you are feeding yourself and your baby." The women cheer, laugh, and hug each. "After a few months, I will give you a little piece of cotton bark root to chew on and your flowers will come."

"Cousin Pearl, you mean we can make us flowers come when we wants?"

"And don't have no flowers if we don't want none?"

"Old Miss Charlotte gon' be beside herself, jus' a tryin' to keep up wid dis un wid chile, dis un ain't wid chile no more."

"After one or two of you, have a" -- I hold my hands to my stomach to indicate a miscarriage --

"I will tell Miss Charlotte that the workload of the pregnant women must be lessened."

"Cousin Pearl, I shore is happy you don come outta de womb agin."

As the women pull straws from my hand, they laugh and tease each other about who will get the chance to have a little bundle first.

~~~~~~~~~~~~~~

Soon enough, I report to Miss Charlotte. "Miss Charlotte, you should be happy to hear that five of our women are expecting a baby. I will be sure to keep a close watch on them."

"That is just perfect, Pearl, keep up the good work."

When I pass Master Ben one day coming from the Big House, he stops and looks at me suspiciously. He frightens me now and I walk home to the quarters stiffly, not turning back to see if he still stands there.

When the women's flowers come on, it is assumed that they have miscarried, at which time I petition Mistress Charlotte for a lessened workload and larger food rations. All of the women in the quarters share the extra portions of food given the pregnant women, and the women faking pregnancies secretly help with the household chores of the others.

~~~~~~~~~~~~~~~~

Percy complains about the laziness of the women in the quarters. "All them wenches complaining about being too sick to work cause they are with child, but ain't a one had a baby yet. I believe that Pearl is up to something again. She ain't been the same since that lashing she got." He begins nosing around more than usual.

And he finds what he needs. The ever-vigilant Percy spies two women coming from the cotton field in the middle of the night. In their bags are cotton bark roots.

The Scheme Is Discovered

The bell calls the women of the quarters to the lashing grounds today. I shudder inside and wonder who the victim will be this time and how will I piece together their torn back.

Percy grabs five women out of the group, the five women who have feigned pregnancy. My heart drops, a collective gasp goes up.

I turn to leave, but Percy blocks my path. "You would be getting another lashing yourself if I didn't need you to get these wenches back into the fields. I knew you were up to something. You can't be trusted worth a damn." He directs his words to all the slave women gathered before him: "Don't you listen to her. See what these poor stupid wenches are going to get for being part of Pearl's scheme."

He pulls me out in front. "You women listen! Pearl ain't been the same after that lashing she took, think it messed up her mind, look at her, wearing white head to toe and a head rag." He snatches off the covering. "Well, I be damn, where is all them beautiful locks? Pearl, you done lost your hair and your mind. Don't let me talk to the Master and he have to give you another lashing to bring your good mind back."

I lower my gaze, not in shame for my uncovered head but because I am responsible for the torment that these women will now face. I don't know that I can be who Mina wants me to be and Ruby needs me to be.

The remaining women of the quarters watch, crying and keening as each of the five are tied to stakes; clothing stripped from their backs and given fifty lashes each. We women untie them, and taking turns, carry them to the sick house. We cry as we clean and apply salve to their bloody raw backs. Their shrieks and moans are testimony to misery.

~~~~~~~~~~~~~

I devised the scheme, and the women benefitted from the extra food. But now all the women of the quarters are punished severely for my actions. Percy comes every day to threaten to have me sold. The women must now do their quota of work besides that of the five women who recover slowly in the sick house.

But the strangest thing –– rather than killing our spirits, the beatings, just as with my beating, make our women more determined.

What Percy, the Master, and Miss Charlotte don't understand is that the women are now beholden to Ruby, not to them. Ruby is still here visiting the dreams of the women in the quarters. Last night she came to me and for the first time spoke to me. As usual, she was wearing the red silk dress. She simply said, "Be strong."

A Cruel Threat

Today Master Ben surprises me in the sick house. The welts on my back seem to rise and sting as he speaks. "See you are up and about, Pearl. Be sure you do your work well so that you can stay that way. Hate to have to give you more stripes."

"I understand, Massa Ben. What can I do for you today?"

"First, get any field hand that is ailing back to work as soon as possible. Give them whatever concoction you come up with. Only the sickest should be here." I nod my head in agreement, looking down all the time. "Second, there should be some babies starting in the quarters, find out who may be with child and give her attention every day. Keep a weekly report on each woman for me to see. Let me know what she needs. Pearl, we can't lose any more babies; costs me too much in stock of slaves. I need babies who survive into childhood each year from every woman in the quarters. Need you to let me know when the young girls are ready to start mating."

I am trembling inside. I keep my head lowered.

"Pearl, you do understand, don't you? Hate to put you in the fields. Or worse yet sell you. Miss Emily is too frail to protect you anymore. Do you understand?"

"Yes, Massa, I do understand that the future of this plantation depends on the women in the quarters having babies and healthy babies who can become workers and produce more workers."

"That's right, Pearl; I think you understand me well. Dr. Smith will be here later this week to examine the women whose names you give him. He will work closely with you to make sure nothing goes wrong. And Miss Charlotte wants to be present at each birth."

Mina sits in the corner nodding, pretending to be asleep. When he leaves, she mockingly says, "Dis old woman may be blind but she ain't def. Pearl, you got a choice to make, gal. Got to keep makin' Massa happy and crossin' Ruby or let me teach you how to please 'em both. Dis old woman won't live too much longer, so will you let me learn you more what I and Abena know?"

"Yes, Mina, I am ready," I say, more than eager to learn it all this time.

On Sunday morning, the minister preaches a sermon on obeying our master. He looks out at the enslaved gathered before him, stretches his hands up to heaven and begins.

"According to the Holy Bible, you are to obey your earthly masters with the respect and eagerness to please that you would our dear beloved Christ Jesus. It is your Master's desire that you produce and fill the plantation with precious little children. Do not be led by false pride, superstition, and ungodliness to sin against your Master or Christ Jesus. We know that sin begets punishment here on this earth and in the fiery pits of hell. Know the joy of having many little ones, pleasing your Master and pleasing God Almighty."

I watch as the women shift in their seats. I wonder if the sermon will make them lose their rebellious spirit. But it is what happens next that seals the fate of Bellamy's plan to have the enslaved women produce more children. Sarah's only two boys who survived to be teens are lifted by their shirts by Percy and brought to the veranda, along with the two oldest sons of Peter and Sadie. The parents jump up with scared eyes. The women hold their hands covering their mouths. "These four fine young bucks will be sold at auction tomorrow," says the Master. "And we will sell off children each month if necessary if there are no pregnancies carried to term. The only way that you will replace your sold children is to have more. No more of these perverted miscarriages. Do you hear me?" he screams. Sarah and Sadie rush to Master Ben wailing and on bended knees plead with him not to sell their sons.

"Oh, Massa, please, Massa Ben, dese boys don't do nuthin' wrong. Dey good workers."

"Please, Massa, dey all I gots in dis worl'," pleads Sarah.

The men of the quarters bow their heads in shame and the women weep.

Then the cruelest reminder of the power that he holds over us is voiced. "I know all of you remember, just a few years ago, when old Butler sold every nigga he owned at the Race Track in Savannah." Chills ripple through the crowd; fear, anguish, and grief are visible on the faces of everyone in the quarters as they recall the bitter agony that those enslaved had suffered; the break-up of families, the anguish of separation. It was March 1857, when the largest sale of human beings in the history of the United States took place. For two days rain fell as 436 men, women, and children were auctioned off by Pierce Butler to pay off debts. We called it the "weeping time."

"If you do not have children, I will be forced into the same position as Butler -- you and your families will be sold. You will never see your children, or each other, again."

Not only does Bellamy threaten the break-up of families, but he demands that no more than three women be together in any cabin or place at one time. Only Lizzie and I are to be in the sick house. The sick house becomes off-limits to the women in the quarters until they are called to assist with a birth.

The crowd sits silently until dismissed. Again, as on the day that Ruby hung herself, there is no picnic after service. The families gather their food and belongings and go dully back to their cabins.

Sowing and Reaping

To ensure pregnancies in the quarters, Percy informs us that he will pay visits to violate the women and Master Ben himself will watch couples engage in sexual acts. This is indeed weeping time on Bellamy Plantation.

I am awakened by loud banging and the cries of a young woman. Lizzie runs to open the door. Standing there drenched in sweat with tears flowing is the young house girl Cissy.

"Quick, let me in. I must tell you something," she gasps. "Bertha the cook sent me to warn the women. Lucy heard Master Ben and the men talking. They are all drunk, saying awful things." Cissy starts to cry uncontrollably.

"Talk to me please, Cissy, what do we need to know?" I ask impatiently as I grab Cissy's shoulders. "Lizzie, please get Cissy some water and wipe her face." To Cissy I say, "Sit here on the side of my bed, honey, and try to relax." I pat a spot on my bed.

Cissy takes a deep breath and starts to cry again.

"Cissy, I can't help the women unless you tell me what is about to happen," I say sharply.

"Master Ben and de udders...."

"How many others?"

"Dere's sebben ob dem who come for a supper meetin'. Dey starts drinkin' and talkin' filty talk. Talk filty about de wimmin in de quarters. Say dey gone do some sowin' tonight in de quarters so Master Ben can reap him some nigga babies in de spring. Be just like harvestin' cotton. Dem nigga babies be born almost ebby day. Say he loss hisself tons of money when all dem babies die. Don't believe no fever kill all dem babies the first time, and he know de women was up to sum ting wid so many miscarriage, so he gon make sure dem wimmin in de quarter make up fo his loss."

I finally release the breath I have been holding and grab Cissy's hand. Chills run up and down my body and my heart races. I swallow hard and get the words out. "Okay, Cissy, thank you. We will alert the women. You slip back to the Big House. Be careful." I hug her tightly.

"What are we going to do, Cousin Pearl?" sobs Lizzie.

"Go to Auntie Mina's, tell her what has happened. She will know what to do. Bring her here. On your way back, stop at Auntie Ama's and have her send two girls to each house to warn the women that the men are coming. Then have all of her girls come to the sick house."

Mina arrives, jars and crocks and dog fennel root in a basket. She mixes a concoction of pokeberry juice and castor oil that will within a few minutes give the girls the runs.

"Bring de girls here. I have somethin' for dem. Dem debils won't be able to hurt 'em." Mina lines the young women and the just–ripe girls up for a dose of her mixture.

"Open wide, don't taste good, but better dan what you could git." Frowning and rubbing their lips in dread, each girl takes a gulp of the concoction. "Tell Auntie Ama to tell dem men y'all got de runs."

The girls have just returned to their cabin when the sounds of drunken men stumbling and running into each other are heard.

"Come on out, wherever you are. I want me a nigga wench tonight," they yell as they stagger down our street. I go to the window to see them banging on doors and barging into cabins. The first cabin belongs to Joe and Sallie. I can hear Sallie's screams and the cries of her children.

"Please, please don't, Massa," she cries. "Massa, my husban' and my chillen right here. Please, Massa, please." A gruff voice belonging to one of the two men who entered the cabin yells, "Go outside and stay there until we finish." He pushes the children out of the door. Joe is made to stay and watch while his wife is raped.

Across from Joe and Sallie live Boy and Susie. Two men break into their cabin. Screams of the woman and the cries of children can be heard throughout the quarters. I step back into my cabin and drop to the bed. I let out a big sigh. "Thank you, Abena," I say. "You have saved me again. And thank God old Miss Emily is still alive." My body shakes as I sit stony faced.

The concoction given to Lizzie and the girls starts to take effect. One by one, two, then three, they run into the bushes to relieve themselves. Mina sits on my bed and softly stokes my head. We hold each other, waiting for the sowing to be over.

We both jump when we hear the men next door banging on Auntie Ama's door looking for the three young girls who live with her and help her care for the babies and children.

"I want me a virgin, come on out," we hear one of the men yell.

"Dey not here. Dey sick. Dey at de sick house. Been sick all week everybody dere gots de runs sumtin awful," replies Auntie Ama.

"I don't believe you, old woman. Where are they?" We hear him come out of the back door; in the weeds are the girls, squatting and moaning in pain as their bowels run uncontrollably.

"Phew, nasty niggas," he yells as he runs to join his disheveled drunken buddies who are singing and staggering back to the Big House. Mina and I wait for the girls. They return ashen and weak but unmolested. They surround Mina and hug her tightly. The cabin reeks of vomit and bowel discharge, but we hold each other, cry for ourselves, and for the violated women, their powerless husbands and children.

Mina turns to me and says sternly, "Chile', you knows what we got to do now." I nod.

~~~~~~~~~~~~~~~

Mina calls the water girls to the sick house this morning after the sowing. They are told to give each woman who had been raped a dog fennel root to chew and swallow the juice. This will stop conception or produce an immediate abortion.

Mina Crosses Over

We have not seen Mina today. She did not go to the kitchen house to pick up her basket of food especially saved for her. Kizzie is sent to take the meal to her. When she enters Mina's cabin, Kizzie sees her still in bed peacefully asleep, but she is unable to wake her. She rushes to the sick house.

"Cousin Pearl, come quick, something is wrong with Auntie Mina."

I follow Kizzie to Mina's and as I enter a feeling of dread overcomes me; my stomach sinks and I know that Ruby coming to me in the dream was a warning. I know as I walk in that Mina is dead. I kneel at her bedside and kiss her lined forehead.

I dismiss Kizzie so I can be alone with Mina. I kiss her scarred and calloused hands, witness to years of picking cotton. Her body now lifeless and cold appears even frailer, so old. The power that emanated from her tongue and unseeing stares is no more. I kiss her sunken cheeks, for she is my mother -- she has birthed me into a new life. I weep for the loss of my mother and feel shame for the years of fearing and resenting her.

"Mina, please forgive me. Forgive me for believing that you were trying to take my Ruby from me. We both loved her. I could not see that you loved me, too."

I sit next to her bed in peace until Bina and Hannah come in to help me bathe and dress her for burial. We send her black dress to one of the women to wash and ask Bertha for a clean white apron from the kitchen house. We cover Mina's bald head with a clean red scarf.

Tonight, the quarters come to pay their respects. Men, women, and children bid farewell and wish Mina a good journey home. Two men volunteer to make a coffin for her burial. I sit with her the rest of the night.

~~~~~~~~~~~~

This funeral in the quarters is occasion of sorrow and joy. We mourn the departure of the old African woman, but the grief of the quarters is muted by our knowledge that she is free of the burden of bondage. Stolen as a young girl, Mina spent her life a slave. Tonight I learn that she too as a young girl had a spirit of rebellion, like Ruby. She was blinded after several attempts at running away.

The procession starts at Mina's cabin. Two by two we walk behind the coffin carried on the shoulders of Mingo and Joe. We walk slowly through the dark woods carrying pine torches. The men lower her coffin. On top of it we place the clay pots, a cauldron, feathers, and bunches of herbs from Mina's cabin. I bury Ruby's bouquet of dried lavender with her. We march around the grave three times. Then each man, woman, and child picks up clods of dirt and throws it on the grave until it is covered.

The men and children return to the quarters, but we women stay to place objects on her grave; a broken pitcher, a piece of broken glass, seashells, and the brightly colored quilt from her bed.

As we are about to leave the gravesite, Bina, Auntie Ama, and the other women encircle me. Each places a kiss on both my cheeks and says, "Bless you, Iya." I am told the word for *mother.* My eyes flood with tears, overcome by the honor and the responsibility. I realize a succession of place and power has just occurred. I have now replaced Mina as the mother to the women. I am honored and I am afraid.

Power of the Womb

As soon as the weary women come in from the fields today, Lizzie is dispatched to tell them to meet at midnight at Ruby's grave. The women understand the risk they take in participating in the womb rebellion; they, their husbands, or children could be sold as an act of retribution. Our actions have to be carefully calculated.

Tonight we gather around Ruby's grave, but we call upon the great mother, Yemaya, the protector of pregnant women and guardian of midwives. I lead the chant, the same one in the strange language I had heard when I was enclosed in the womb of my cabin. "Yemaya Assessu, Assessu Yemaya, Yemaya Olodo, Olodo Yemaya." The circle in which we sit is illuminated by the light of candles inserted in carved spaces in a large watermelon. We chant for what seems like hours; suddenly Alice goes into a trance, her eyes roll back into her eyelids, her body stiffens and she begins to speak. From her lips comes Ruby's voice.

"Every woman in the quarters capable of bearing a child will eventually become pregnant but I will not allow the babies to live to be enslaved. You will not bear the pain of child birth to then bear the pain of watching your child abused or sold. It is better that he or she remain in the spirit world.

"As you carry the baby, you are to rub your belly constantly but gently and whisper, 'Fly spirit fly.' The spirit within you will understand. When the women of the quarters assist with the births, as you wash and oil the child, each woman is to hold the baby close to her heart and whisper into its ears, 'Fly spirit fly.' You are the possessors of your wombs. And of your secret. Tell no husband or child. You hold the power of your wombs. No slave child can ever again be born to live and suffer on Bellamy Plantation. If you follow my instructions, I will never come again. I will leave you in peace. As you will be giving peace to your offspring."

I leave the meeting in deep turmoil. Preventing births is one thing but how can I stand by and let innocent babies die? It is my duty as midwife to bring healthy babies into the world and to nurture them after birth. What Ruby is requiring tears into my heart like a sword. Abena told me that in Africa, every woman was required and expected to perform the motherhood function, to do her share to ensure that the human race continued. In bondage, having children and having a family is the way that we know

300

we are human, have human sensibilities that the slave masters deny that we possess.

Tonight I pray for guidance. I fear the wrath of Bellamy, that he will follow through on his threat. The greatest fear in the quarters is to be sold off and separated from one's loved ones. Bellamy encourages the women in the quarters to have children for two reasons; it increases his stock of slaves, and it is a threat held over the quarters to behave or else.

But I also fear Ruby's rage. The quarters have paid a dear price for neglecting to bury her properly and to appease her angry, wandering spirit. The quarters has paid a large price for my insisting that Ruby ever be born. As I am drifting off to sleep, I appeal to Yemaya, protector of pregnant women and guardian of midwives, to come to me in a dream.

And she comes. In the dream, Yemaya stands near the ocean. She wears a flowing, elegant dress of intense blue, and a necklace of blue beads adorns her throat. She speaks to me in the loving and caring tones of a mother, like Abena, like Mina. "All babies are the spirits of ancestors reborn; I am first of all the protector of ancestors. You will care for the mothers, and birth the babies, you will not talk about it or tell anyone why as the babies do not live beyond the nine days. The babies will return to the spirit world to be reborn again -- and again -- until they are born free."

I awake with grateful tears, knowing that it is the right way, for I am now assured that even though babies will die, their spirits will come again to a time when it is safe for them to be born. The belief of old will abide in this terrible land. As I take a deep breath, a sense of freedom sweeps over me. I feel an immense peace. There is no fear, no fear of Bellamy, of Ruby, only peace. From the power of my own womb will be created and birthed a spirit of rebellion on Bellamy plantation that will endure. The old way of Afrique will now be unleashed.

~~~~~~~~~~~~~~~

The first baby is a boy born to Maude and George. Dr. Smith and Miss Charlotte scrutinize everything I do as I deliver the baby, a perfectly healthy birth. The first to hold the baby after the mother is Sarah, still grieving for her lost boys. She holds the infant as close to her heart as possible and whispers, "Fly spirit fly" into his ear. The baby is passed to Bina who washes him, holds him close to her heart and whispers, as does Hannah who greases him and dresses him. The healthy baby boy dies on the sixth day after his birth. Throughout the year, each month, a baby or babies are born on Bellamy plantation, always under the watchful eye of Dr. Smith and Miss Caroline. Not one baby lives more than nine days. I continue to report to Bellamy as I know Miss Charlotte and Dr. Smith do. I continue to provide the best care for the pregnant mother as his wife and doctor watch our every move. It is a mystery that Dr. Smith, Miss Charlotte, and Bellamy cannot figure out. The women on Bellamy plantation pretend that they too cannot figure it out. Their babies continue to die. They mourn. But they are strong. To prevent their children from becoming slaves has become their mission, their life. Their belief system is so strong that the babies die. It is a sad time at Bellamy Plantation. But underneath it all is a rightness, a kind of secret joy that each woman holds to herself.

The War Years– 1861–1865

Enslaved women having babies has become the last thing on Master and Mistress Bellamy's mind. After April 12, 1861, life will change forever on Bellamy Plantation. And not only for the enslaved but for Master Ben and Miss Charlotte. When the Confederates fire on Fort Sumter in Charleston Harbor on that day, what is let loose is the whirlwind. The servants in the Big House find every excuse to come to the quarters to let us know the latest news. As we suspect, when South Carolina secedes from the Union, war follows. At last.

Finally, freedom, I hope.

And if not freedom in the full sense, we slave women of Bellamy Plantation are about to get what Ruby called "a little snatch" of it.

As soon as the War Between the States begins, Master Ben takes all the able-bodied slave men with him to construct batteries and coastal defenses to protect Sullivan Harbor into which most of the slaves on his plantation, including Abena, had been brought from Africa. The women of the quarters are put to work spinning cloth, making uniforms, and knitting socks for the Confederates. In addition they are left to take care of the cotton, the animals, the other crops and their families. Percy remains to ensure that the field work is done properly. However, after the attempted rape of one of Auntie Ama's girls, he dies mysteriously, just falls right over into his dinner plate and never wakes up. So now, only the women of the quarters, the house servants, Miss Charlotte, Betsy, and old Miss Emily are left at Bellamy.

Today, all of the slave women are called to the back lawn. The Confederate troops have come to tell Miss Charlotte that the plantation has to be evacuated. Only one male and one female slave can stay. Miss Charlotte chooses Jacob the butler and me to remain behind. All of the women and the old men are told that they must pack to leave. Miss Charlotte also issues orders that everything from the storehouse and the smoke house must be packed to take, as well as directing the house servants to hide precious silverware, china, and crystal. "Don't want them Yankees to get nothing from this plantation," she cries.

The women grumble on the way back to the quarters and strike a defiant tone.

"Let her go, we don't know what dat's gonna be like. Maybe worse dan here."

"I wants to see how dis war ting gonna turn out."

"Wid she gone and Percy gone, we gots freedom here."

"Why should we leave? We de ones who make dis place."

"Yeah, we plow de fields, make de crop."

"We tend de animals, milk de cows, cure de ham, and make de sausage."

"We be free jus' by ourselves."

"De graves of our family and our chillen be right here."

"I say we gedder all de food and take it to de woods, so no Johnny Reb can have it."

By dusk, the women have decided not to go. They work late into the night to hide the food from the storehouse and the smokehouse in the woods.

~~~~~~~~~~~~

I meet Miss Charlotte and Jacob at the Big House early this morning. Miss Charlotte is beside herself with fear.

"Oh, Pearl, something dreadful has happened. All of the house servants are gone, even Bertha and Kizzie. Where can they be? They

307

promised to be by my side during this awful time." She becomes even more anxious when she notices I am alone, no women are with me.

"Pearl, where are the women? Where are the supplies that they have packed?"

I lie. "A bunch of those awful Yankees came last night and spirited off all of the women. I am surprised you didn't hear all the commotion."

"But, Pearl, why didn't you warn me?"

"Miss Charlotte, I was too scared. You know how you told us they would rape all of the slave women and sell us to Cuba. I just stayed in hiding."

"They made the women clear out the entire storehouse and the smokehouse. Took all the food, even made the women kill chickens, and took off with some of Master's cows and goats. It was terrible."

"Ma'am, it is time for us to go," says one of the Confederates.

"Jacob and Pearl, please take good care of Bellamy; don't let those Blue Coats have anything. Protect Bellamy with your lives," says a weeping Miss Charlotte, helping the feeble Miss Emily into the coach.

"We will," say both Jacob and I in unison.

The soldiers and Miss Charlotte, Betsy, and her mother-in-law leave Bellamy.

~~~~~~~~~~~~~~

Tonight, Bellamy is a lonesome place. The women still hide in the woods, and Jacob is at the Big House. I am alone in the sick house. I look out on the row of oak trees that witnessed our enslavement and to the spot where the Big Oak once stood that even in its absence gives testimony to the spirit of a young woman whose heart and mind could never be enslaved. I think of Ruby as I drift off to sleep, and she comes to me.

I ask, "Ruby, why couldn't you be patient, stay a little longer. See? The War has begun. You and your baby would be free."

Ruby answers, a smile on her face. "Pearl, what I did was as much for you as for me and my baby. I had to free you. If you wonder what Mina and I talked about all those years, we talked about freeing you. You are free now. As are all those babies who never had to become slaves. They can all come back now, be birthed in freedom."

~~~~~~~~~~~~~~

We teach ourselves fishing and hunting animals for food; we plant our gardens, and we delight in communal meals. We abandon the cotton fields altogether. We are bound by a new measure of sisterly love. Despite hardships, we have endured. Through the power of our wombs we created the means by which to defy.

The Union soldiers come today. The War is ended. We make a feast and celebrate our freedom with them. The women now wait for their men to come home. We are told that General Sherman says that we can stay on the Bellamy land that we occupy. The afterbirth of generations of enslaved are buried under trees on the land. Our grannies and aunties are buried here, our men, our children. Despite bitter stories, we have memories of love and kindness and laughter among us. This is the place we call home.

The lavender field remains, as well as the tales of a young pregnant woman wearing a red satin dress with a daisy in her hair walking through the woods.

Epilogue

Today is my final visit with Mrs. Lancaster. She says she has one last thing to share with me. Her face is aglow as she excitedly tells me," You might find it an interesting addition for your story.

"I delivered more babies the first year after the war than I had ever delivered," she boasts. "It seemed that every month, a baby was being born. The women from Bellamy plantation who once did not have a baby live past nine days soon had toddlers running all around.

"In January 1866, fourteen babies were born to the women and girls who had been enslaved on Bellamy plantation. Ten of those were girls." She hands me a slip of paper.

Girls Born to Women Formerly Enslaved on Bellamy Plantation in January 1866.

January 12: Ruby Louise

January 13: Ruby Ann

January 23: Ruby Sarah

January 25: Ruby Alice

January27: Ruby Jane

January 28: Ruby Frances

January 28: Ruby Elizabeth

January 30: Ruby Grace
January 30: Ruby Beatrice
January 31: Ruby Pearl

I feel tears spring from my eyes. "This is amazing," I say as I read the final name. My aunt Ruby Pearl. Mrs. Lancaster grabs me by the arm and looks me directly in the eyes. "You see, it wasn't me, it was Ruby that changed the women, made them know their power. I was just the midwife."

Carrie Telfair

CPSIA information can be obtained
at www.ICGtesting.com
Printed in the USA
FSHW01n1749240818
51620FS